AND JUSTICE FOR ALL?

"This is terrible, most terrible!" Pepin said in his animated way. "The Indians in this country are too brazen, too vicious. They deserve to be hunted down and made to pay."

"By now the war party might be many miles away," Shakespeare said.

"So?" Pepin touched the tomahawk at his belt. "In Canada we would never let such a foul act go unpunished! It boils the blood to think about it!"

Nate, busy starting a fire, looked at the fiery trapper. "If it's the same bunch I saw, there are nine of them and only four of us. We'd be committing suicide if we went after them."

"Are we yellow?" Pepin said gruffly. "I say we teach these savages a lesson and get back all of the hides and horses that were stolen. I say we kill each and every one of the braves responsible."

Nate, with a sinking sensation in the pit of his stomach, saw that his real troubles were just beginning.

The *Wilderness* series:

#17
WILDERNESS
TRAPPER'S BLOOD

David Thompson

LEISURE BOOKS NEW YORK CITY

A LEISURE BOOK®

June 2004

Published by

Dorchester Publishing Co., Inc.
200 Madison Avenue
New York, NY 10016

ISBN 0-8439-3566-9

Visit us on the web at www.dorchesterpub.com.

#17

WILDERNESS

TRAPPER'S BLOOD

To Judy, Joshua, and Shane.

Chapter One

Life was good.

Or so rugged Nathaniel King decided as he rode along the bank of a gurgling stream high in the pristine Rocky Mountains. A free trapper by trade, young Nate had just completed the spring trapping season, and as proof of his skill there were 175 prime beaver pelts bundled on the three pack animals trailing his big black stallion.

Nate was already imagining how he would use some of the money he would get at the upcoming Rendezvous when he sold his plews. At the going rate, he stood to earn upwards of 900 dollars, and that was for just the hides he had collected on this trip. During the preceding fall trapping season he had acquired 210 prime hides which were safely stored in his remote cabin. Added to his current haul, he'd leave the Rendezvous with 1900 dollars, minus however much he spent for fixings such as powder, ammunition, new traps, grub, and the like, and what his wife spent on whatever struck her womanly fancy.

In a day and age when the average mason or carpenter made less than 500 dollars a year, Nate reflected that he was doing right fine. He was justly proud of his ability to provide for his family, and looked forward to the look on Winona's lovely face when she learned he would finally go along with her plan to buy a fancy rug for their home. She had been pestering him about it for quite some time, ever since he made the mistake of taking her to St. Louis and letting her see how white women lived. Since then he'd been persuaded to install an expensive glass pane in their window, to board over the dirt floor, and make a few other changes that Winona felt improved their homestead.

Women! Nate thought, and snorted. Men were unable to live without them, yet living with them was sometimes as trying as living with a cantankerous grizzly. Still, as he fixed his wife's shapely form in his mind's eye and dwelled on the many grand times they had shared, he realized he wouldn't trade being married for all the plews in the world.

The black stallion suddenly nickered, shattering Nate's daydream. He promptly reined up, hefted the heavy Hawken in his left hand, and gazed in all directions, seeking whatever had caught the stallion's notice. No mountain man survived very long being careless, and Nate had every intention of living to a ripe old age.

The streams Nate had trapped were situated on the west slope of the Rockies, well to the north of his usual haunts. No one Indian tribe claimed the territory, yet many hunting and war parties passed through the area regularly. Some of them were Blackfoot, Piegan, and Blood war parties, all of whom would slay and scalp a white man on sight. Nate had to constantly exercise the stealth and caution of a panther if he hoped to see his family again.

Nate was at the edge of a dense pine forest. Before him unfolded a spacious valley lush with green grass. Beyond the valley reared a solitary mountain crowned by a jagged peak tipped with snow. On the slope of that mountain figures were moving, riders moving from north to south. He counted nine, and although the distance was too great to note details, he felt certain they were Indians.

For one thing, there were no packhorses, which whites invariably had. For another, the riders were strung out in single file, a customary practice of war parties whether mounted or afoot. And finally, sunlight glinted off what could be the tips of several lances.

Nate stayed right where he was to avoid being detected. The trapping had gone so well he hated to risk spoiling it by tangling with hostiles. He thought of his four friends, free trappers like himself who had entered the region with him and then scattered to various points to lay their trap lines, and he hoped none of them had encountered the band.

It took five minutes for the Indians to cross the mountain slope and disappear in fir trees. Nate waited another five before jabbing his heels into the stallion's flanks and moving down the valley. Warm sunshine on his bearded face and the cries of sparrows, jays, and ravens served to relax him and reassure him that the danger had passed.

During the eventful years Nate had spent in the wilderness, he had learned to read Nature as some men read books. When the wildlife fell silent, he knew to expect trouble. When the animals frolicked and chattered, all was well. The habits of the birds and beasts, the moods of the fickle weather, and the rhythms of the wild in general were as familiar to him as his own countenance in a mirror.

Often Nate's knowledge had meant the difference between life and death. The Rockies were no place for the squeamish, the weak, or the ignorant. Those who didn't learn fast paid for their laziness with their lives. Of the hundreds of hopeful greenhorns who entered the mountains each year, the majority never got to return to the States.

Not that Nate ever would anyway. He had grown to love the untamed frontier, to revel in a life of freedom unmatched by anything back East. Here he could do as he saw fit, accountable to no one but himself. There was no boss standing over his shoulder, telling him how to go about his work. There were no deceitful politicians trying to rule his life with their petty laws and rules. He was truly as free as the eagle, ruled by nothing but his heart's desire. Could any man ask for more?

Nate shook his head and grinned. He was becoming too wrapped up in his own musings for his own good. Staying alert was the key to staying alive, so he kept his eyes on those fir trees on the mountain until he reached a point abreast of a gap in the hills to his left. Toward this he made his way, knowing that in the next valley over he would find one of his four friends.

The blazing morning sun climbed to the midday position, and still Nate forged on. Weeks had elapsed since last he had talked to another human being, and he was eager for company again. Loneliness was part of a trapper's life, a part he had become accustomed to, but unlike some trappers who preferred to be alone the whole year through, Nate couldn't wait for companionship when the trapping season was over.

A red hawk soaring high on uplifting currents caught Nate's attention. He watched it glide over the hills, and spotted a magnificent black-tailed buck in a clearing on one of them. Had the range been shorter, he would have been tempted to drop the deer.

Nate's nostrils tingled to the rich, dank scent of bare earth as he entered the gap. Here little sunlight penetrated. He saw many tracks of elk, bear, and deer, but only four sets of horse prints, and they were so old they were barely visible. He knew who had made them, and he grinned in anticipation.

The next valley was narrower but contained more vegetation. At a ribbon of a stream dotted with large beaver ponds, Nate turned to the left to follow the waterway to his friend's camp. He covered two miles, then caught the faint acrid scent of smoke. A little further on he saw a clearing ahead, and to one side, under the spreading branches of a towering tree, a small fire crackled. Four horses were tethered nearby, but there was no sign of their owner.

Halting, Nate cupped a hand to his mouth and hailed the camp, a practice that prevented those with itchy trigger fingers from making a fatal mistake. "Shakespeare! Where the devil are you?"

"Right behind you, Horatio."

Startled, Nate shifted in the saddle and glared at the speaker. "You ornery varmint," he declared, feigning anger. "Don't you know any better than to go sneaking up on someone?"

Shakespeare McNair threw back his white-maned head and laughed lustily. Then he made a grand show of bowing at the waist, declaring, "So please your majesty, I would I could quit all offenses with as clear excuse as well as I am doubtless I can purge myself of many I am charged withal."

"Let me guess," Nate said, and deliberately guessed wrong. "*Romeo and Juliet?*"

"Pitiful. Downright pitiful," the older man grumbled. "What are the young'uns coming to nowadays? Didn't you have a proper education?" He came alongside the stallion. "That was from *King Henry the Fourth*. Part One, if I'm not mistaken."

"I'll take your word for it," Nate said. He had long ago discovered the folly of arguing with his mentor over the

works of William Shakespeare. No one, absolutely no one,
knew the writings of the Bard better than the grizzled
mountain man whose nickname was a token of his peculiar
literary passion. Shakespeare could quote his namesake by
the hour, and to Nate's knowledge no one had ever proven
a single quote to be wrong. "But what's this nonsense
about you having an excuse for scaring the daylights out
of me?"

"'Tis true, young sir," Shakespeare said good-naturedly.
"I was only helping to keep you on your toes."

"You needn't worry in that regard," Nate said, moving toward the tree. "The war party I saw earlier did the
trick."

"What war party?" Shakespeare asked. He was somber
now, since he well realized the implications, and he listened
attentively while Nate described the band. "Blackfeet would
be my guess. This is one of their main routes south to Ute
country."

"My thinking too," Nate agreed. Dismounting, he tied
his horses, then walked to the fire, and was handed a tin
cup brimming with steaming coffee. "They're long gone
by now, though. We can be well on our way before they
return."

"I suppose," Shakespeare said. Squatting, he poured himself a cup, and quoted thoughtfully, "Nimble mischance,
that art so light of foot, doth not thy embassage belong to
me, and am I last that knows it?"

"In other words, we shouldn't let down our guard for a
minute," Nate translated.

"Exactly." Shakespeare sipped loudly and stared at the
bundles on Nate's pack animals. "Appears to me you did
right fine."

"How about you?"

"One hundred and ninety-four plews."

"You beat me again."

"Did I?" Shakespeare grinned. "Well, I had to work my britches off to do it. Must of scoured the valleys and parks westward for better than forty miles."

"The same here." Nate sat back against a log and took a swallow. "The beaver are becoming harder and harder to find. Each season it gets a bit worse."

"And it will continue to get worse," Shakespeare predicted. "There are just too blamed many trappers. Why, not ten years ago, before the fancy ladies and fashionable gentlemen back in the States took to craving beaver hats and collars and such, there were so many beaver in these mountains that a man couldn't kneel down to take a drink without bumping heads with one. The critters chopped down so many trees to make their dams, there was hardly any timber left to use for making firewood."

"Oh, please," Nate said, chuckling. "I'm no longer a child."

"Don't believe me if you want," Shakespeare responded. "I only exaggerated a little." Sighing, he encompassed the neighboring mountains with a sweep of an arm. "There's been a lot of change since the trappers moved in, and not all of it has been for the better. If things keep going the way they are, before you know it we'll have settlers spreading out over the countryside like a swarm of locusts, driving off the Indians and killing off all the game. Out here will be just like the East." He shuddered. "God help us."

Nate shook his head. They had been over the same subject countless times, and nothing he had said had been able to convince McNair that the prairie and the mountains would last forever as glorious bastions of freedom and adventure. Most Easterners wouldn't think of crossing the Mississippi; they regarded everything west of that mighty river as wasteland, part of the Great American Desert, as explorer Stephen H. Long had called the plains during his brief expedition some years before.

"I hope I don't live to see that," Shakespeare was saying. "I want to remember the wilderness as it should be, wild and uninhabited."

"It must be all your white hairs," Nate joked. "You've turned into a first-rate worrier."

Shakespeare fixed his narrowed eyes on the younger man. "Your mind is all as youthful as your blood," he quoted, adding, "You'll learn, though, One day you'll see that I knew what I was talking about."

Their banter was suddenly interrupted by a crackling in the woods to the northwest. Nate leaped to his feet, his right hand dropping to one of the twin flintlocks adorning his waist. In addition to the pistols, he had a butcher knife in a beaded sheath and a tomahawk tucked under his wide brown leather belt. Slanted across his broad chest were the powder horn and ammo pouch for his guns.

McNair had also risen. "It's him again," he muttered.

"Who?"

"The same contrary cuss who has visited my camp every few days for the past month. If I had any sense, I would have shot the nuisance weeks ago."

"Who are you talking about?" Nate asked, tensing as the crackling grew louder. Vaguely, he spied a bulky form moving toward them through the heavy undergrowth.

"Not who," Shakespeare corrected him. "What."

The brush parted, revealing a young black bear, a male no more than a year old, if that. It squalled on seeing the camp and came forward at a lumbering shuffle. McNair's horses showed no reaction; evidently they were accustomed to the bear's visits. But Nate's animals whinnied and fidgeted.

"Stand still until he gets to know you," Shakespeare advised. "I don't want you spooking poor Brutus."

"Brutus?"

"Well, I couldn't very well call the thing 'It' all the time, now could I?" Shakespeare responded testily. Setting down his coffee, he moved around the fire and stood with his hands on his hips. The bear displayed no fear whatsoever as it came right up to the mountain man and rubbed its head against his buckskin-clad leg. "See? As friendly as a Flathead." Shakespeare stroked the creature's neck and scratched behind its ears.

"You're getting awful softhearted," Nate said. "Wait until I tell our wives."

"We can't go around killing every animal we see," Shakespeare countered. Reaching into his possibles bag, he pulled out a thin strip of jerked deer meat, tore the piece in half, and gave it to their visitor. The bear knew just what to expect, and delicately took the dried meat between its tapered teeth, then chomped hungrily.

"Are you fixing to take Brutus back with you?" Nate asked.

"Not hardly." Shakespeare gave the bear the rest of the jerky. "This coon might be softhearted, but I'm not as addlepated as you'd like to think."

Nate studied the bear a moment. "That's a nice hide you're passing up. And all that meat and fat. It makes my mouth water just to think about it."

"Oh?" Shakespeare glanced up, triumph lighting his face. "Would you kill that pet wolf your son is so attached to?"

"Blaze? Never."

"Then don't be poking fun at Brutus." Shakespeare patted the bear's front shoulders and the animal flinched and whined. "What's this? What have we here?" Shakespeare leaned down, examining the fur. "Looks like something got its claws into you."

Nate bent over the bear for a look. There were three slash marks, so fresh blood still seeped from them, each at least an inch deep. "Panther, you figure?" he asked.

"Could have been," Shakespeare said, although his tone implied he was not quite convinced. Straightening, he surveyed the primeval forest, particularly the various shadows under some of the giant pines. "There aren't many creatures that will tangle with a bear, even a small one like Brutus."

"Another bear would," Nate mentioned casually.

"True," Shakespeare said, his lips puckering.

The object of their concern was now rummaging in the stack of supplies at the base of the tree, sniffing loudly as it poked its black nose under the flaps of closed parfleches and into whatever other nooks and crannies it could find.

"Your friend just makes himself to home, doesn't he?" Nate asked.

Shakespeare had been deep in reflection and had not noticed. Uttering a squawk, he bounded at Brutus and gave the bear a swat on the rump. "You pesky bottomless pit! You'll wait until I fix some biscuits for supper."

"You still have flour left?" Nate marveled. "I ran out weeks ago."

"There's an art to conserving grub," Shakespeare boasted. "When you have as many gray hairs as I do, no doubt you'll be almost as good at it as I am."

"White hairs. Your hair is white. How many times must I remind you?" Nate said. "And now that you mention it, yes, I would like to be as old as these mountains."

"Most shallow man! Thou worms-meat, in respect of a good piece of flesh indeed! Learn of the wise, and perpend: civit is of a baser birth than tar, the very uncleanly flux of a cat. Mend the instance, shepherd," Shakespeare stated.

Chuckling, Nate walked to the black stallion and began stripping off his saddle. "If it's all right with you, we'll start after the others at first light."

"Fine."

"I wonder how they've fared?"

"Pointer and Jenks will be lucky if they have a hundred pelts between them. They're as tender as the soles of a baby's feet and as ignorant as granite."

Nate glanced over his shoulder. "I had no idea you held such a high opinion of them."

"Don't misconstrue my remarks, Horatio. I like them despite their shortcomings or I wouldn't have agreed to having them join our party." Shakespeare was keeping his eyes on the black bear, which had wandered to the other side of the clearing and was sniffing at the remains of a rabbit Shakespeare had skinned and eaten the day before. "They're young, but they're sincere. They truly want to be good trappers. And if they live long enough, they will be."

"What about Pepin?"

"That feisty *voyageur* might beat us both." Shakespeare stroked his beard. "He's about as skilled a woodsman as you're ever likely to run across."

"To hear him talk, he's the best."

"That's a *voyageur* for you. I haven't met one yet who didn't love to flap his gums just to hear himself talk."

Nate laughed. Canadian trappers were a colorful, hardy breed who lived each and every day as if there would be no tomorrow. He'd known others in his time besides Pepin, some as friends, others as enemies, and there was no denying they could hold their own against any free American trapper alive.

"I'm mighty curious about what brought him here," Shakespeare commented. "If I've heard him say he loves the North Country once, I've heard him say it a thousand times. It's odd he'd leave it for the southern Rockies."

"You figure he got into a fight and killed someone and had to make himself scarce?"

"That would be my guess, but this child isn't about to pry into another man's personal affairs."

Nor would Nate, although he was as curious as his mentor. The only fact Pepin had revealed was that he had been a *coureur de bois* up north, which roughly translated to a ranger of the woods, or the Canadian counterpart of an American free trapper. The rest of the man's past was a complete mystery.

"Enough about him," Shakespeare said. "What say we go hunt ourselves a deer and make dog of the critter? I have coffee left too. If I throw in some biscuits and berries, we'll have a feed fit for royalty."

"Count me in," Nate said, his stomach grumbling at the mention of food. "Just give me a moment to set my pelts aside." He swiftly unloaded his pack animals and placed the plews beside McNair's. His possibles bag, which had been hanging from his saddle, was draped over his shoulder and angled across his chest below his powder horn. He then checked his rifle and the pistols.

The Hawken was fairly typical of those widely used by company men and free trappers alike. Made by the renowned Hawken brothers of St. Louis, it boasted a 34-inch octagonal barrel, a set trigger, accurate sights, a ramrod housed under a metal rib, a heavy butt stock, and a butt plate in the shape of a crescent. Powerful enough to drop a bull buffalo, it was .53-caliber. A half-ounce lead ball and 214 grains of black powder were the standard load. Nate's flintlocks were both .55-caliber, smoothbore single-shots. At close range they were as effective as the Hawken.

"There's a small lake west of here," Shakespeare said as he retrieved his rifle. "Deer like to hole up near it during the day. It shouldn't take us no time at all to track one down."

"All we need is some wild onions and I'll . . ." Nate immediately stopped talking when he saw the young black bear suddenly rear up on its hind legs and sniff noisily, swiveling its head as it tested the air. "What's gotten into Brutus?" he asked.

Shakespeare looked and frowned. "He must have the scent of something."

The bear took a few awkward steps, then dropped onto all fours, spun, and sped off into the underbrush, plowing through the vegetation as if in fear for its very life.

"Maybe it's time you took your annual bath," Nate joked. He turned, laughing, and happened to gaze in the direction from which Brutus had approached the camp earlier. Every nerve in his body tingled and a shiver rippled down his spine when he saw another bear standing 20 yards off Only this one wasn't a black bear.

It was a full-grown grizzly.

Chapter Two

There wasn't a trapper alive who had more experience with grizzlies than Nate King. By a curious quirk of fate it had been his lot to run up against the fierce beasts time after time, which had resulted in his earning the Indian name of Grizzly Killer. Among the Shoshones, his adopted people, his prowess as a slayer of grizzlies was almost legendary. Yet ironically, as Nate was often the first to admit, usually he had prevailed more by accident than design.

Nate regarded the great brutes with deep respect, if not outright dread. Whenever he saw one, if possible he made it a point to head the other way just as fast as his legs or his mount could carry him. The times he had been forced to fight were those where no other recourse was open to him.

Such as now.

The sight of the grizzly lumbering forward was enough to cause the bravest soul to flee, but Nate stood his ground. He knew how destructive grizzlies could be, how they would wantonly tear apart everything they found in a trapper's camp, and he could ill afford to let that happen. There were his horses and supplies to think of, not to mention the pelts he had worked so hard to gather. So, firming his grip on the Hawken, he took a few strides, putting himself between the grizzly and his plews. "Shakespeare," he said urgently. "We have more company."

The older man whirled. "Damn! Now we know what took a swipe at Brutus!" He moved up beside his young friend, admiring the determined set of Nate's jaw. At times such as this, Shakespeare was proud to have been the man who taught Nate all there was to know about wilderness survival. Shakespeare had known many frontiersmen over the years, but none had taken so naturally to the arduous life than the one he fondly regarded as the son he had never had. "If he charges, go for the head," he cautioned.

"A heart shot is better," Nate said. Having carved up a lot of grizzlies for their hides, he'd seen firsthand that their brains were protected by enormous skulls as well as layers upon layers of thick muscles.

"We can't get a good heart shot from head-on," Shakespeare noted.

"Try for the eyes, then."

The grizzly slowly advanced as they talked. It had its ponderous head low to the ground, its nostrils quivering, as if it was still on Brutus's scent. Steely sinews rippled under a lustrous coat. Long claws glinted in the sunlight. Here was the most massive killer known on the North American continent, its height at the shoulders being five feet, its length over seven feet, and its weight in the vicinity of 1500 pounds. A huge hump, characteristic of the species, bulged above the front shoulders.

The horses had seen the bear and were working themselves into a frenzy, snorting and stomping and tugging at their tethers.

"On my cue," Shakespeare said, tucking his rifle to his right shoulder.

"Wait," Nate said. "I want to try something." He would rather run naked through a briar patch than have to fight another grizzly. In desperation he resorted to a tactic that worked on lesser beasts, but which he had never yet witnessed do any good against the terrors of the Rockies; he took a long stride, lifted his arms, and screeched like an enraged banshee while jumping madly up and down.

The effect on the grizzly was interesting. It halted, a paw half raised, and stared at the screaming human. Never had it beheld the like, and in the depths of its dull mind it didn't know what to do. It wasn't afraid, since fear had no meaning to a creature capable of shredding an elk's neck with a single blow. Instead it was puzzled, as it would be if it came on the spoor of an animal it had never seen before. Humans were familiar to this bear as timid things that fled at its approach. The antics of this one, though, were so different as to give it pause.

Nate jumped higher, yelled louder. He flapped his arms, hoping against hope he could drive the grizzly off and avoid a bloody clash.

The bear lowered its foot and glanced from the humans to the horses and back again. It had never tasted the flesh of either and so was not impelled by its stomach to go after them. And since 90 percent of its actions were motivated by its belly, the grizzly began to depart, to go find quieter morsels, but as it did, the wind shifted and abruptly the grizzly registered the tantalizing scent of rabbit blood. Blood of any kind always had the same effect. Instantly the bear's mouth watered and there were rumblings in its paunch, the age-old signal for the grizzly to do one thing and one thing alone—attack.

Shakespeare's keen eyes saw the bear's front claws digging into the soil. "Look out!" he shouted. "Here it comes!"

As if shot from a cannon the grizzly hurtled straight at them, moving with astonishing speed for such a heavy animal. When aroused, grizzlies were capable of moving as fast as a horse, and this one was a credit to its kind.

Nate was sweeping the Hawken level when Shakespeare's rifle boomed. The bear's head jerked, blood spurted from its brow, but it never slowed a whit. Nate sighted on the monster's right eye, then realized the grizzly would be on them before he could fire. "Move!" he cried, and did exactly that, leaping to the left just as the bear raced between them. Perhaps dazed by the lead ball, it made no attempt to claw them, but barreled into their supplies and pelts, scattering belongings every which way.

Pivoting on a heel, Nate aimed as the grizzly slid to a halt and turned. The beast was broadside to him for a few seconds, all the time he needed to fire into its chest, going for its heart.

At the retort the grizzly arched its spine and roared, its mouth agape, its lips curled up over its fearsome teeth. Seared by acute agony the likes of which it had never felt before, the bear focused on the cause of its pain and charged again.

Nate had his back to the tree. In pure reflex he tossed the Hawken aside and drew both pistols, cocking the flintlocks as he did. The bear was coming for him like a bolt of furry lightning. He had no time to think. He had no time to plan. All he could do was what he did, fire both pistols at point-blank range and vault to the right. His shoulder was struck a resounding blow that tumbled his head over heels. His head hit a stone or other hard object, and for several seconds the world was spinning like a child's top. When the spinning ceased he was lying on his back, the empty flintlocks clutched tight, while directly above him was the hind end of one of the horses.

"Son, are you all right?"

Strong hands gripped Nate's shoulders and assisted him in sitting up. Blankly he stared at the grizzly, lying slumped on its stomach next to the tree, blood oozing from the holes where its eyes had been. The impact had partially cracked its skull, and a bubbly froth was trickling from the fracture.

"I reckon the damn thing killed itself," Shakespeare declared. "Busted its own head wide open." He cackled and gave Nate a smack on the arm. "I never saw the like."

"Me neither," Nate mumbled. Grunting, he slowly stood.

"How many does this make now?" Shakespeare asked.

"I've lost count."

"Wait until the Shoshones hear. You keep this up and they're liable to start thinking there must be something supernatural about you."

"Don't be ridiculous."

"You know as well as I do that Indians are not only deeply religious in their own way, they're awful superstitious too. They're forever calling on the Great Mystery or the Great Spirit for help, and they believe in things like guardian spirits, animal spirits, and such." Shakespeare paused. "Course, we do pretty much the same thing, only we call on God and believe we're looked after by guardian angels. When you think about it, the white and the red cultures are more alike than most realize."

Nate walked to the dead giant and shook his head in amazement at his deliverance. By all rights he should have been slain. Once again Providence had seen fit to spare him, although he had no idea why. Sinking onto the log, he worked at reloading the pistols and his rifle. After a while he realized his friend was staring at him and he looked up. "Yes?"

"What's bothering you, son? You're a mite flushed."

"Wouldn't you be after what just happened?" Nate extracted the ramrod from his rifle. "These close scrapes always leave me flustered. My blood is pumping so hard I can practically hear it."

"Which is perfectly normal." Shakespeare sat down and began reloading his gun. "Why, I recollect the time I was up in the geyser country, hunting elk. I shot a big old bull and tracked his blood trail deep into the woods. Hadn't no more than set down my rifle and drawn my butcher knife than there was this terrific roar and a grizzly twice the size of this one came rushing toward me out of the brush."

"Twice the size of this one?" Nate asked skeptically.

"This took place when I was about your age," Shakespeare said, unruffled. "Bears were bigger back then."

"The tall tales must have been bigger too."

Shakespeare arched an eyebrow. "Do you want to hear this yarn or not?"

"I'm all ears."

"All right then. Anyway, there I was, standing next to this dead elk with just my knife in hand, and here came this snarling grizzly. It was too close for me to try and run away, and there wasn't time for me to scoop up my rifle, take aim, and shoot."

"So what did you do?" Nate asked when McNair stopped.

"That's the strange part. To this day I don't know what made me do what I did." Shakespeare made a show of fiddling with his ammo pouch.

"Which was?"

"Well, before I tell you, you have to keep in mind that this here bear was coming straight toward the front of the elk. And what I did was, I grabbed hold of the top antler and lifted with all my might, raising the head and the whole rack clear off the ground." Shakespeare gazed off into the distance. "That elk had the biggest rack I ever did see."

"And? And?" Nate prompted.

"Why, the darn fool bear couldn't stop and ran smack into the antlers. Must of knocked me a good twenty-five feet. When I sat up, there wasn't a scratch on me. And there was that grizzly, stuck fast with those antlers ripped deep into its neck and face. The noise that thing made! It spooked every creature for fifty miles."

"Did the bear die?"

"Not then. It tore loose and went off into the trees without another look at me. The thing was bleeding like a stuck pig. Likely bled to death later on, but I didn't go see."

"Your point?"

"My point is that I was so rattled I sat there shaking for the better part of an hour. Just shook and shook like an aspen leaf, and nothing I did helped." Shakespeare smiled. "Being scared is nothing to be ashamed of. Every man is at one time or another. It's how you handle the fear that counts. In that regard, you have no cause to be ashamed."

"Thanks," Nate said sincerely.

Shakespeare studied the kill. "It would be a shame to let a fine specimen like this go to waste. I suppose we'll have to spend the rest of the day skinning it." He smacked his lips. "Which isn't all that bad a proposition. Painter meat can't shine with this, but meat is meat to a hungry man and I've always been rather fond of bear steaks myself. How about it?"

"Bear meat will do fine."

So the remainder of the afternoon and evening was devoted to dressing the grizzly. Its hide was removed intact, and Shakespeare insisted on having Nate take possession since

Nate, as Shakespeare put it, "was the one the bear seemed to like the most." Since they had no caskets in which to put the oil, they left that task unattended. Shakespeare made a point of carving out the heart, which was as big as the heart of a large ox, and added it to the thick slabs of meat they had selected for their supper.

"Ever eaten bear heart, son?"

"Can't say as I have."

"I'll share with you. Heart meat is a delicacy too delicious to pass up. Got hooked on it once up in Flathead country when I shot a deer that was in poor order. Sickly thing it was, and the meat was terrible. But I was starving and needed to eat something, so I roasted the heart and some of the other organs." Shakespeare scrunched up his face. "The liver about made me gag, but the heart was so tasty I wished I'd had five or six more. Ever since I've been a heart man."

"I'll bet you're partial to tongues as well."

"As a matter of fact, I am," Shakespeare responded. "Buffalo tongue in particular. The first time . . ." He broke off, his eyes narrowing. "You danged upstart."

"I beg your pardon?" Nate said innocently.

"Don't play dumb. You landed a broadside fair and square, and I'll take my licks without complaint." Shakespeare laughed lightly, then quoted, "I am a very foolish fond old man, fourscore and upward, not an hour more nor less. And to deal plainly, I fear I am not in my perfect mind."

"I could have told you that."

"Twice! Twice!" Shakespeare clutched at his chest. "You wound me to the quick, young sir! And to think that you were weaned at the nipple of my wisdom!"

"William Shakespeare wrote *that*?"

"No. I just made it up. Wasn't it grand?"

Both men roared.

That night, seated by the crackling fire, warm and with a full belly, Nate listened to his mentor read from the thick book McNair never went anywhere without, a rare collected edition of the famous playwright's works. This night Shakespeare read from *Hamlet*. Later, after they had turned in and Nate was on his back, his head propped in his hands and staring thoughtfully at the myriad of sparkling stars, he asked, "Do you think Hamlet did the right thing?"

"In what respect? Treating Ophelia as he did? Acting mad? Which?"

"Neither. In taking so long to decide what to do. If he'd killed the king outright, he would have spared himself a heap of grief."

"Think so?" Shakespeare shifted, his eyes almost luminous in the glow of the fire.

"Don't you? All that agonizing was a waste. When a man sees that something has to be done, he should go out and do it and not worry himself to death over it."

"If only life were that easy," Shakespeare said wistfully.

Nate was to have bitter occasion to remember his words later on, but for now he closed his eyes and drifted into an undisturbed slumber that lasted until the chirping of sparrows awakened him well before dawn. Throwing off his buffalo robe, he rose and went into the bushes. He yawned loudly, scratched his thick beard, and was hitching at his leggings when he saw something which instantly brought him fully awake.

A gray wolf sat on a knoll ten yards away staring curiously at the two-legged oddity that wore the hides of deer on its body and the fur of beaver on its head. The faint scent of roasted meat had brought the wolf close to the camp, but its natural wariness had prevented it from drawing any nearer.

Nate's first reaction was to reach for a flintlock. Then he hesitated, sensing the wolf was no threat. Feeling exposed with his leggings down around his knees, he quickly finished adjusting them and tightened his wide leather belt. When next he looked at the knoll, the wolf was gone.

Forest creatures were that way. Ordinarily they lived quiet lives, going about their daily routines as stealthily as they knew how, the predators because without stealth they would rarely catch the prey they needed to sustain themselves, and the prey because if they made too much noise they might attract the unwanted attention of a predator. There were exceptions, as there were to every rule. Grizzlies often plodded along heedless of the noise they made; they had no natural enemies, and they ate anything and everything that caught their eye, from roots to wild fruits to living things.

Nate reflected on this as he strolled back to his bedding. There were those who would view him as peculiar for having forsaken the security of life in New York City for the savage uncertainties of the mountains, but he would not give up his life in the wild for all the gold in the world. The element of constant danger added a certain zest to a man's life, and made him appreciate each and every moment of his life that much more.

"Morning, Horatio," Shakespeare greeted him.

"About time you got up. You're turning into a lazy layabout," Nate said, nodding to the east where the first pale rays of the rising sun were visible. "Half the day is wasted."

"When a man has lived as many years as I have, he's entitled to sleep in late once in a while."

Within half an hour they had broken camp and were riding northeastward at a slow pace so as not to tire their fully laden pack animals. Nate had the lead, the Hawken across his thighs. "Refresh my memory," he said at one point. "Is it Jenks or Pointer we collect next?"

"Pointer, I do believe," Shakespeare said.

"Let's hope he remembered that we agreed to head on home about this time and he has all his traps in."

"If he doesn't, no harm done. We'll lend a hand." Shakespeare skirted a pine. "It's easy to lose track of time out here. One day is so much like the rest that they all become a blur after a while."

"Until the first snow."

"True enough."

Their course took them toward a row of stately mountains whose majestic peaks reared to the very clouds. High up a steep, rocky slope they climbed, to a pass which would take them to a lush valley. They were well into the sunlit pass when Nate spotted impressions in the ground and abruptly reined up. "I don't like the looks of this."

"What is it?" Shakespeare called.

Swinging down, Nate knelt and examined a series of unshod hoofprints made within the past week or so. "Indians," he announced. "Seven or more, heading into the valley."

"Maybe it was the same bunch you saw," Shakespeare guessed.

"Maybe," Nate said, although he doubted that was the case. The band he'd seen had been heading due south. This party had been going due north, days ago. If it was the same band, then for some reason they had turned around at some point and swung a little to the east, then made to the south. Such aimless meandering made no sense. Rising, he stared at the end of the pass. "What concerns me most is whether they spotted Pointer."

"We'd better hurry. And keep your eyes peeled."

The mouth of the pass widened out onto a curved shelf overlooking the valley proper. Here Nate halted to scour the countryside. A bald eagle was soaring over the high grass flanking the blue stream, and to the east several cow elk were browsing. No smoke marred the scenic picture, nor was there any sign of Pointer's camp.

"He must be at the west end of the valley," Shakespeare said.

A serpentine game trail brought them to the valley floor. Nate was riding on the south bank of the stream when he saw hoofprints in the soft earth at the water's edge. Halting, he checked, then declared, "It's the same bunch. They went this way."

"Damn."

At a trot they proceeded into dense timber, now and again coming on more of the week-old tracks. At length they came to a beaver pond. The dam showed evidence of recent repair. Close by the opposite shore was a large lodge, and as the two trappers watched, a young beaver swam from the shore to the lodge and disappeared under the water with a slap of its flat tail.

"This would be the first place I'd lay some traps if I was trapping this neck of the woods," Shakespeare said somberly.

Nate poked his heels into the stallion. He was growing more concerned by the minute, and he prayed his fears were unjustified. He thought of Harold Pointer, an amiable 18-year-old from Illinois, and of Pointer's parents, who were patiently waiting for their son to return with the money they needed to save their farm from the auction block, and he wanted to curse but didn't.

Shakespeare was equally anxious about the young trapper. He'd known literally hundreds of hopeful greenhorns who had come to the Rockies bound and determined to make their fortunes in the fur trade, the majority of whom had wound up dead, victims of their ignorance and their brashness. He always tried to warn them. He always stressed the hazards a trapper faced. But whatever he said invariably went in one ear and out the other. They were young; they were full of vim and vinegar; they were invincible, in their estimation; and they knew better than some old geezer who sported more wrinkles than a dried prune. The only way they would learn was the hard way.

A clearing materialized ahead, so Nate slowed and placed a thumb on the hammer of his Hawken. He glimpsed a black circle that had to be an old campfire, but no other sign that anyone had ever been there. Stopping at the tree line, he slid off the stallion and tied his horses to low limbs. Then, rifle leveled, he walked into the open. There were horse tracks everywhere. And footprints. Nate bent down to inspect a set, turning as he did, and involuntarily stiffened when he heard his mentor bellow.

"Behind you!"

Straightening, Nate spun as the brush erupted in a flurry of crackling and snapping.

Chapter Three

Ordinarily Shakespeare McNair was not the jittery sort. With his age had come wisdom, and in his wisdom he had learned that every now and then life offered up unpleasant surprises and there was nothing any man could do to avoid them. They had to be taken in stride, met calmly and overcome patiently. Every living person had to swallow the bitter with the balm and pray everything worked out in the end.

Staying composed when under pressure was a trait Shakespeare prided himself on. So he was more than a little embarrassed when, because of his abiding affection for his companion, he blurted out a warning on seeing the undergrowth across the clearing move without first verifying there was a threat. For out of the brush, flapping mightily, popped a large raven.

Nate held his fire when he saw the black bird take wing. It uttered an irritated squawk as it banked above his head and soared off up over the pines. On passing above him the raven dropped something from its big beak, and the object fell almost at Nate's feet. He glanced down, not knowing what to expect, but certainly not expecting to see a grisly, stringy eyeball dotted with peck marks. A human eyeball, no less. "Dear Lord!" he breathed, and hurried to the spot where the raven had first appeared. Extending the Hawken barrel, he parted the weeds.

First to hit Nate was the awful stench. Gasping, he turned his head aside long enough to gulp fresh air, then leaned forward to stare at the partially decomposed body of Harold Pointer lying sprawled on its back. Pointer had been stripped naked and mutilated. His stomach had been torn open and his innards ripped out and left draped over the ground. His throat had been slit wide. And there were other things that had been done, unspeakable things only the most diabolical of minds could have conceived, horrible things no human being should have to see.

"The poor kid," Shakespeare said over Nate's shoulder. He had seen worse in his time, but not much worse.

"About five days or so ago, you figure?" Nate asked, holding his breath so he could edge a bit closer and search the surrounding area. Not a single one of Pointer's clothes was anywhere around. Every last article the man possessed had been stolen.

"About that," Shakespeare said, backing away to scan the clearing. "I'll find which way they went."

Nate also backed away until he could breathe freely again. He tried to remember the exact town in which Pointer's folks lived so he could send them word of their son's death, but for the life of him he couldn't recall what it was. "We should bury him," he remarked forlornly.

"Whatever for? Let Nature take its course," Shakespeare said from over near the stream.

"He deserves a burial. He was our friend."

"If he hadn't started to rot away, I'd agree," Shakespeare said, looking up. "There isn't much I'm squeamish about, but touching rotten flesh is one of them."

"Then I'll plant him myself."

Shakespeare sighed. "Hell. You and your principles. All right. I'll help. But don't blame me if I'm a mite whiffy for a spell."

The burial was a nightmare. Since they lacked proper digging implements, they resorted to thick limbs sharpened at one end to pry apart clods of earth. The ground was hard, the chore grueling, raising blisters on their palms and fingers. But the digging was a picnic compared to the job of getting the corpse from the weeds to the hole. Nate tried grabbing an ankle and pulling, but the soft flesh was like mush in his grip and he wound up with gory bits clinging to his hand. Shakespeare came up with a better idea; they used the limbs to flip the corpse over and over until they rolled it into the grave. Then they took turns covering the body so that neither of them would become too queasy from the smell.

"There," Nate said when the last bit of loose dirt was on the pile. "Now he can rest in peace."

"You do know, don't you, that some animal is likely to come along, dig him up, and make dog of him?" Shakespeare said.

"No matter. We'll have done what we can. That's all that counts."

"Not quite," Shakespeare said. "There's still the matter of the bastards who did this." He returned to the stream and squatted, scrutinizing the tracks. "They're a canny bunch, I'll give them that. After doing their dirty work, they rode smack into the water. The current has long since washed away their prints so there's no telling if they went back out the valley the same way they came in or whether they continued on to the west."

"That's odd."

"What is?"

"I've never heard tell of a war party going to so much trouble to hide their trail before. Indians are proud of the coup they count. Sometimes they leave sign just so others will know who did it."

"Maybe these were shy," Shakespeare said.

"Or maybe," Nate declared, "they knew there were more trappers in this region." His eyes met his mentor's, and without another word they hurried to their horses, mounted, and headed back down the valley until they came to a creek that fed into the stream. This they followed northward for over five miles, into a verdant paradise in the midst of a ring of towering peaks.

"Jenks should be here somewhere," Shakespeare said.

"If the war party didn't find him too."

Anxiously they searched, going up one stream and down another, always on the lookout for hostiles. They were nearing a fork when Nate spied a stretch of churned-up earth, and as he trotted forward his stomach muscles tightened. The hoofprints were so plain there was no mistake. "Seven riders. Three or four days ago."

The tracks took them to the northwest, to a meadow. They were still a ways off when Shakespeare spotted a telltale black circle in the grass near the water. "Did they make that fire, or did Jenks?"

Nate galloped to the site, and was off the stallion before the horse stopped moving. Touching the charred pieces of wood confirmed the campfire was days old. He discovered a number of moccasin prints of different sizes, and deduced that considerable activity had taken place.

Shakespeare had gone to a nearby cottonwood. "Here's

where Jenks had his horses tied," he said, indicating a line of hoofprints and patches of flattened grass where the animals had bedded down at night.

"But where is he?" Nate wondered, fearing the worst. Hawken in hand, he walked in a loop, probing the high grass for the body he was certain must be there. When he found nothing on his first sweep, he conducted others, widening the loop each time. He canvassed an area 50 yards in diameter, and was both relieved and puzzled when the hunt proved fruitless. "Maybe they took Jenks with him," he speculated as he walked up to Shakespeare.

"Could be. The Blackfeet, those scoundrels, like to take captives to their villages to impress the women and the sprouts. They hold grand feasts, and the high point of their festivities is when they torture their captives to death."

Nate was already painfully aware of the Blackfoot custom. Once he'd fallen into their hands and been forced to run a gauntlet, to dash between two rows of armed warriors, an ordeal which he had barely survived.

"The tracks go into the stream again so we can't follow them," Shakespeare said.

"We have to see about Pepin," Nate said urgently. "If they haven't gotten him yet, he has to be warned." They both mounted and rode in a northeasterly direction. Dense timber proved a frustrating barrier, slowing them down, and it was late afternoon by the time a new mountain range hove into sight. Nate, again in the lead, was emerging from cover into the open when the glint of sunlight off metal in the high grass 60 yards away gave him a fraction of a second in which to throw himself from the saddle. He heard a rifle crack, even as he yelled, "Take cover!"

Shakespeare had not been caught napping. He'd seen the gleam of light almost at the same time and sprung from his white horse. Keeping bent at the waist, he glided through the grass to where Nate was crouched. "You hit?"

"No. Whoever it is rushed his shot." Nate stared at their horses, which had scattered but not fled far.

"It could be one of the warriors in the war party," Shakespeare said. "We'd best kill him quick and make ourselves scarce before the rest show up."

"You go left, I'll go right," Nate proposed, then did so, hugging the ground and parting the grass with exquisite care. He hadn't gone more than 20 yards when movement to his left alerted him to someone creeping in the opposite direction, directly between McNair and him. It had to be the one who had shot at them, he realized. The man was making enough noise to rouse the dead, cracking dry stems underfoot and brushing loudly against every blade of grass he passed.

Nate flattened and crawled to intercept the creeping figure. Either the ambusher was incredibly careless, he reasoned, or the man was in an almighty big hurry. He couldn't believe an Indian would act so stupidly, not when from earliest childhood warriors were taught how to use supreme stealth when necessary. A buckskin-clad form materialized. Nate froze, let go of the Hawken, and slowly drew his tomahawk.

The figure was pumping his limbs furiously, apparently trying to reach the horses.

Digging in his knees and toes, Nate waited until the man was directly abreast of his hiding place. Then, venting a Shoshone war whoop, he leaped up and pounced, aiming a terrific blow at the figure's head. In the nick of time he recognized the startled, upturned face below him and managed to swerve the tomahawk just enough to one side to miss the man's skull.

"King!" the man blurted out.

"Jenks!" Nate responded, appalled at how close he had

come to splitting the greenhorn's head in half. "What the hell are you doing taking a shot at us?"

"I didn't know," the younger man declared, sitting up. Perspiration beaded his smooth brow. He was a lean youth, only 17 years of age, with square, bony shoulders and knobby knees. His brown eyes brimming with moisture, he pushed upright and exclaimed, "Thank God! Thank God it's you!"

From out of the grass a few feet behind the greenhorn rose Shakespeare, wearing a wry grin. "I can't say I think much of the way you greet your friends."

"Forgive me," Jenks said, smiling idiotically at both of them. "I didn't stop to take a good look. I just saw riders coming and figured it was them."

"Who?" Nate asked, although he already knew.

"I never saw them clearly," Jenks said, and unexpectedly commenced shaking, trembling from head to toe.

"Are you all right?" Shakespeare inquired. He put a hand on the young man's arm and could feel the arm quiver.

"Just glad is all." Jenks exhaled loudly while holding out his quaking hands. "I reckon I'd better sit down." He sank onto his buttocks and stared at his rifle. "To think I almost killed one of you!"

"Shucks. You never came close," Shakespeare said to relieve the greenhorn's anxiety. "You were aiming at Nate, but I think you hit a squirrel over in the next valley."

Laughter burst from Jenks, nervous laughter, the kind typical of a person so overwrought he desperately needed to release his pent-up emotions.

Nate squatted and waited for their trapping partner to fall silent. "Why don't you tell us what happened?" he prodded. "Talking might help calm you down."

"There's not much to tell," Jenks said. "Three days ago, about sunset, some men showed up at my camp. I'd been off gathering the last of my traps, and was late getting back. It was almost dark, and when I first saw them through the trees I figured it was you coming to fetch me as we'd agreed. Then I heard voices, but I couldn't quite make out what was being said or even what language it was. I stopped and tried to get closer, but I must have made some noise because the next I knew one of them let out a yell and took a shot at me and five or six of them came running toward me." Jenks licked his lips. "I don't know how the hell I got out of there in one piece. All I remember is dropping my traps and running until I couldn't run any further."

"Did they come after you?"

"I should say they did! I'd collapsed on a log when I heard them moving through the pines behind me." Jenks shook again. "So I snuck off and spent the next hour working my way up the valley until I was sure they had given up." He paused. "The next morning I went back and they were gone. So were all my pelts, all my gear, all my horses, everything."

"At least you're alive," Shakespeare said. "Which makes you a far sight luckier than Pointer."

"Harry?" Jenks said in alarm, gazing all around. "I just noticed. Where is he? What happened to him?"

"The same band that tried to kill you got to him first," Nate explained. He didn't deem it appropriate to go into much more detail. "We buried him earlier."

"Oh, God," Jenks said, blanching.

"Don't fall to pieces on us, Lester," Shakespeare advised. "We all need to keep our wits about us because the band might still be in this area."

"What do we do?" Jenks asked stridently.

"Shakespeare and I will rearrange our packs and free up one of the pack animals for you to ride," Nate said. "Then we have to check on Pepin." He noted the position of the sun. "It's too late to reach him today. We'll have to make camp in an hour or so and go on in the morning."

"Is that smart? I mean, shouldn't we push on through the night?"

Nate shook his head. "Riding at night is dangerous enough without having a string of packhorses to keep an eye on. And the trail Pepin took is one that would give a bighorn sheep second thoughts."

"I just hope we reach him in time," Jenks said.

"You're not the only one."

Nate tossed and turned all night long. Occasionally he would lie and listen to Shakespeare's snoring and marvel at the mountain man's iron constitution. In the morning he was up first, and had all the horses ready to go before the other two woke up.

The cocky Canadian had insisted on trapping an extremely remote area, so secluded there was only one trail in and out and so high up the temperature dipped to near freezing at night even in the spring. The game trail was easy enough to locate, but the ascent, winding up a series of switchbacks with sheer cliffs on one hand and steep rock walls on the other, was nerve-racking. At times barely enough space existed for the horses to walk, and Nate would peer down at the boulder-strewn ground hundreds of feet below and try not to imagine what it would be like to fall and be dashed to pieces.

Eventually the trail brought them to a plateau abundant with wildlife. Elk, deer, and bighorn sheep sign were everywhere, and lesser animals were constantly sighted.

Nate had no sooner cleared the crest than he saw a spiral of gray smoke a half mile off. Was it from Pepin's fire? he asked himself. Or had the war party beaten them there? He waited for his companions to join him, then held out his lead rope to Lester Jenks. "I'm riding on ahead with Shakespeare. You come on after and bring all the packhorses."

Jenks blinked. "I don't much like the notion of being left behind."

"If the war party is already here, we can't very well out-run them hauling our pack animals along," Nate explained. "This way, if Shakespeare and I see it isn't safe, we'll gallop back and let you know not to come on in."

"What if there's a fight? I'll miss out."

Nate almost grinned. This from a man who had never once fought Indians? "If there are hostiles, and if they spot us, you'll have more than your share of fighting. Trust me." Handing over the rope, he rode forward at a walk until Shakespeare came alongside him. Together they brought their mounts to a gallop.

"I don't see any tracks yet," Shakespeare mentioned, surveying the ground.

A grassy field brought them to a thick forest, through which a crystal-clear stream flowed. They veered into the brush, using the thickets and undergrowth to screen their movements, but stayed within sight of the stream.

The *voyageur* had picked a wondrously picturesque spot for his camp. Nestled in an oval clearing at the base of an aspen-covered slope down which the stream wound like a glassy ribbon, it afforded protection from the wind and plenty of forage for horses. A lean-to had been constructed on the bank of a pool formed by a glittering waterfall. At this high altitude the air was crisp, invigorating. A striking azure sky completed the picture.

Nate spotted the five horses belonging to the Canadian right away, each staked out in the clearing and nipping at the sweet grass. He also saw pelts ready to be transported and supplies piled near the lean-to. All appeared serene, but as Nate had long ago learned, appearances could be deceiving. Reining up behind a spruce, he glanced at McNair. "I'll go on in alone, just in case."

"Why you?"

"I'm younger."

"So?"

"I run faster when someone is after my scalp."

"This is a hell of a note. A whippersnapper like you throwing my age back at me." Shakespeare frowned. "My pulse, as yours, doth temperately keep time, and makes as healthful music."

"Maybe so. But now isn't the proper time to put it to the test," Nate said. Bracing the stock of the Hawken on his leg and holding the barrel so the rifle slanted upward, he went around the spruce and made a beeline for the lean-to. The five horses all looked up, but displayed no alarm. He was within yards of the pool when he heard loud whistling in a stand of pines beyond, a lively tune he knew to be *Mon canot d'ecorce,* or "My Birch-bark Canoe," a popular *voyageur* song Pepin was inordinately fond of singing. Sure enough, a few seconds went by and out of the trees strolled the man himself, bearing an armful of firewood.

Pepin was characteristic of his hardy breed: short, stocky, and as powerfully built as a bull. A red woolen cap crowned his shock of curly hair. He wore a fringed buckskin shirt, which was likewise common among American free trappers, but the deerksin leggings which ran from his ankles to a bit above his knees, leaving his thighs exposed, and the short skirt, or breechcloth, he wore were both distinctly Canadian. So was the red sash about his waist, complete with a large beaded bag that resembled somewhat the possibles bags of the mountain men.

Pepin had no sooner emerged than he looked up, spied

Nate, and broke into a broad grin. "*Mon ami!* Allo! Allo! *Depuis quand êtes-vous ici?*" He ran around the end of the pool, the flat soles of his moccasins slapping on the earth.

"Hello, Pepin," Nate greeted him. "It's good to see you again."

"And you, my friend!" Pepin declared, reverting to English as he dumped the wood by the lean-to and hurried over to the black stallion. "Give us your paw!"

Nate bent over to shake and nearly lost his perch, so vigorously did the *voyageur* pump his arm. It was impossible to know Pepin and not like him, and Nate liked the man a lot. Pepin was so full of energy, so full of life itself, that his robust attitude was often contagious. "How has the trapping been?"

"*C'est formidable!*" Pepin answered. "Just great. I have over two hundred prime pelts."

"Shakespeare was right. I should have known."

"What?"

Sliding down, Nate gazed out over the vast plateau. "Have you had any trouble?"

"Difficulty? *Non!* No." Pepin's weathered brow creased. "Why do you ask, my friend? What is it you are holding back?"

"Just a moment," Nate said. Turning, he waved an arm so Shakespeare would know all was well. Then he draped the same arm over the Canadian's wide shoulders and said, "I bear bad news."

Pepin listened attentively to the story of Pointer's horrid fate and Jenks's misfortune, flushing a deep scarlet the whole while. When Nate finished, Pepin slammed a fist into his open palm and gave expression to a long string of oaths in French. He was still cursing vehemently when Shakespeare and Jenks arrived.

"Thank goodness the murdering devils didn't get to you,"

the youth told the *voyageur*. "We feared we wouldn't get here in time."

"This is terrible, most terrible!" Pepin said in his animated way. "The Indians in this country are too brazen, too vicious. They deserve to be hunted down and made to pay."

"By now the war party might be many miles away," Shakespeare said.

"So?" Pepin touched the tomahawk at his belt. "In Canada we would never let such a foul act go unpunished! It boils the blood to think of it!"

Nate, busy starting a fire, looked at the fiery trapper. "If it's the same bunch I saw, there are nine of them and only four of us. We'd be committing suicide if we went after them."

"Are we yellow?" Pepin said gruffly. "I say we teach these savages a lesson and get back all of the hides and horses that were stolen. I say we kill each and every one of the braves responsible."

"I'm with you!" Jenks cried.

Nate, with a sinking sensation in the pit of his stomach, saw that his real troubles were just beginning.

Chapter Four

Shakespeare McNair also saw the danger in the direction the talk was taking. A full lifetime had permitted him to see rash folly for what it truly was, and since he had no hankering to lose his hair at such a ripe age, he sided with Nate by saying, "It could take us weeks, and there's no guarantee we'd ever find them."

"The effort will be worth it if we avenge the memory of our fallen fellow!" Pepin replied.

Jenks nodded. "I have nothing to lose. They've already got my goods."

"But not ours, nor our plews," Shakespeare said bluntly, "and I don't figure to give them the chance to get their hands on any of my fixings."

Pepin nodded at his own hides. "But that is easily solved, *mon ami!* We can cache all the pelts here with most of the supplies. The extra horses can be let loose to roam as they please since it is doubtful they will try to go down the cliffs by themselves. Simple, *non?*"

"Some of us have families to think of," Nate mentioned.

"Is this the famous Grizzly Killer talking?" Pepin rejoined. "Is this the man I heard so much about I couldn't wait to be his partner? The man the Blackfeet, Piegans, and Bloods consider their greatest white enemy? The man who has beaten the Sioux? The man who saved his wife from a life of captivity among the Apaches?"

"I had no choice in those instances," Nate lamely said.

"And you do now? After Pointer has been slain? After Jenks was nearly killed?" Pepin made a clucking sound. "How can you say such a thing? What about the next trappers who lay their lines in this region? Are they to be butchered and scalped because we did not have the courage to deal with this?"

Such unexpected eloquence caught Nate off guard. He didn't know quite what to say, so he said nothing.

"I'll go with you, Pepin, if no one else will," Jenks said scornfully. "I'm not afraid of any damn hostiles, and I mean to have my things back come hell or high water."

"That is the spirit, my young friend!" Pepin faced McNair. "And you, *Carcajou*? Will you see justice done? Will you join us in our noble cause?"

"Noble causes have a habit of getting folks killed."

"Does that mean no?"

"It means I'll ponder some and let you know when I make up my mind," Shakespeare promised.

"As you wish, *mon ami*."

Pepin produced a short spade from his supplies, and the remainder of the day was spent digging the hole where the hides and other possession would be cached.

There was a certain technique the trappers always employed. First a straight, round hole was dug, usually to the depth of five or six feet. Next a chamber was made adjacent to the hole, a chamber big enough to accommodate all the items to be cached. Afterward, the hole was filled in with dirt. Any excess earth was scooped up and scattered, in this case into the pool. Finally branches were used to rake over the top of the hole and bits of grass and leaves were added to completely cover it. When all was done, only an experienced eye could tell that the ground had even been disturbed.

Nate helped dig, but his heart wasn't in it. He had liked Pointer as much as any of them, and he was as outraged as they were by Pointer's death and the theft of Jenks's peltries. By the same token, he had learned the hard way that vengeance was a two-edged sword; those who sought it often reaped it. He did not care to die without seeing his family again. But—and that word seemed to stick in his throat—he did have an obligation to his trapping partners, a responsibility to do what was best for all of them. It would be selfish of him to think only of his own interests.

By evening most of the stores had been cached. Pepin took Jenks off to hunt supper. Nate strolled to the pool and sat glumly down at the water's edge. He swirled the surface with a finger and saw the reflection of his mentor appear. "Have you made up your mind yet?"

"I was waiting for you to make up yours first."

"I made my feelings clear earlier."

"Did you?" Shakespeare asked, sinking down. "I heard your common sense speaking but not your heart."

"Women think with their hearts. Men don't."

Shakespeare chuckled. "Men like to pretend they don't, but they do. Just as much as women. We just lie about it because we don't like to admit we let our emotions get the better of us." He tossed a pebble into the water. "No man likes to 'fess up to losing his self-control. It makes him seem weak."

"If we go after that war party, we're as dumb as turnips."

"You'll get no argument from me."

"It'd be plain stupid."

"As stupid as anything."

"Who knows when we'd get home?"

"Time would tell."

"It would be a dunderhead thing to do."

"True enough."

"Feebleminded is a better description."

"Then feebleminded it is. Throw in featherbrained, empty-skulled, and doltish too."

Shifting, Nate stared into Shakespeare's kindly eyes. "But we have it to do, don't we?"

"As surely as the sun rises and sets every day."

"Damn."

"That's what we get for being men and not boys. A boy can always make up excuses to get out of doing what has to be done, but a man, *if* he's a man, has to face facts and do what has to be done without complaint."

"Sometimes I wish I'd never grown up."

"Don't we all, son. Don't we all."

Pepin and Jenks returned an hour later with a bighorn sheep. "You should have seen the shot I made," the Canadian boasted. "There was this gorgeous sheep, so high up on the rocks his horns were touching the bottoms of the clouds, and I put a ball through his head with my first shot!"

"Amazing," Nate said dryly, and coughed. "There's something you should know," he continued. "Shakespeare and I have decided to go along." Before he could elaborate, the *voyageur* sprang at him, embraced him in a bear hug, and spun him in circles while whooping like a demented Comanche.

"*Tres bien! Tres bien!* I knew you would! Does a panther run from chipmunks? Does an eagle flee from jays? Does a bear hide from ants? *Non!* Never!"

Nate was spun a few more times for good measure. He couldn't help but laugh when Pepin stepped back. "You're plumb crazy. You know that, don't you?"

"*Oui*. But without a touch of craziness, life can be so dull, *non*?"

"Dull, maybe. Longer, definitely," Shakespeare muttered.

That night Pepin regaled them with exaggerated tales of his escapades in Canada. He told of Lake Winnipeg, "so deep a *coureur de bois* once found a Chinaman floating on the top." And of rivers where the current was so swift, "a man can fire his rifle, paddle a few strokes, and be in position to catch the ball as it comes down." He claimed "the grizzlies in Canada are so big, the full-grown ones you have here are no bigger than their cubs." And after dark had settled, he mentioned the time he found mammoth tracks.

"What the dickens are mammoths?" Jenks asked. "No one ever told me about them."

"That's because no white man has ever laid eyes on one," Pepin said. "And the Indians who have seen the things don't like to talk about the creature because they're mighty bad medicine. The Indians believe that anyone who sees a mammoth will die soon after doing so if the mammoth doesn't kill the person first."

"Sounds like another one of their nature spirit yarns to me," Jenks said.

"Not the mammoth, *mon ami*. The Lillooet, the Bella Coola, the Yuroks, they all say that mammoths are flesh and blood." Pepin pulled out his pipe and tobacco pouch. "And after what I saw, young one, I think they are right." He pondered a bit. "It was eight years ago. I was crossing the Canadian Rockies through Yellowhead Pass when I saw these peculiar tracks. The Indians with me went into a panic and begged me to leave the area before the thing found us."

Nate, although he well knew that telling tall tales was an established tradition around campfires at night, and suspected the *voyageur* was having fun at the greenhorn's expense, was prompted by curiosity to ask, "What were the tracks like?"

"*Strange.* Very strange," Pepin answered as he tamped tobacco into the pipe bowl. "They sank over four inches into the packed snow, where our tracks sank less than an inch. Each one was as long as both of my feet combined. There were no claws, just toes."

"Toes?" Jenks asked skeptically.

"Toe prints just like those you or I would make, only five times bigger," Pepin said.

The youth snorted. "If I ever see prints like that, I'll know I've had too much to drink."

"*Peut-etre.* But I was sober. And I know what I saw."

The conversation turned to other topics. Nate stretched out on his blankets, making himself comfortable. The events of the day had left him fatigued, and he had no trouble at all in falling asleep. So soundly did he sleep that he was shocked when, on feeling a firm hand shaking his shoulder, he opened his eyes to find the rosy rim of the sun already crowning the eastern horizon, setting the sky ablaze with a riot of color.

"Getting a mite lazy, aren't you?" Shakespeare said.

Coffee was already boiling. Pepin had taken the horses to the pool and was watching them drink. Only Jenks hadn't yet quit his bedding.

"I'll let you do the honors with the greenhorn," Shakespeare said, grinning. "That way you won't feel so bad."

"Thanks," Nate grumbled. Sitting up, he stretched and thought of the task they had set for themselves, hoping they weren't making the gravest mistake of their lives. Despite the justness of their cause and the necessity for doing it, he couldn't shake lingering doubts. He made no mention of his feelings to the others. Why bother, when he had given his word he would go and it was too late to back out?

Breakfast consisted of leftover meat from the night before. They were in the saddle before the sun rose completely, and making their way down the escarpment before the morning was an hour old. The previous night they had decided to head for the spot where the war party had last been seen. Consequently Nate was again in the lead. Anxious to overtake the hostiles as soon as possible, he kept the black stallion at a trot until nearly midday.

After a short rest, they pushed on. Few words were exchanged. This was serious business, and not a man among them, including the usually rowdy Pepin, was in a mood for small talk.

By going over certain ridges rather than around, and by taking a shortcut Shakespeare knew of, they were able to shave hours off the journey. Even so, they didn't arrive at the particular mountain slope Nate sought until shortly after noon on the second day. Once there they spread out, seeking sign, and it was Shakespeare who first found the trail. At a whoop from him the others converged and sat staring at the hoofprints.

"Well, I suppose we'll find these vermin soon enough," Jenks said rather nervously.

"Within four or five days would be my guess," Shakespeare commented.

"And then we will have some new scalps to show off at the next Rendezvous, *non*?" Pepin declared happily.

"You plan to lift their hair?" Jenks asked in horror.

"But of course!"

"But that makes us just as bad as them."

"Bad?" Shakespeare interjected. "Do you think that what this band did makes them any worse than we are?"

"Certainly," Jenks said. "We're not murdering savages."

"Neither are they," Shakespeare responded.

The greenhorn was incredulous. "How can you say such a thing, McNair? They butchered Pointer, stole everything I own."

"We don't know yet whether the Blackfeet or the Bloods or some other tribe is to blame, but it doesn't matter. Every one of them has made no secret of the fact that white men are their enemies. In their eyes, we're trespassers, invaders who are killing off all the beaver and a lot of other game and spreading our diseases among them wherever we go. In their eyes, they're doing what they think they have to do to protect their people, what they believe is right."

"That doesn't make it so!"

"As you go through life I think you'll learn that being right or wrong, good or bad, often depends on which side of the fence you're on."

"Are you saying that you excuse what they did to Pointer?"

"I wouldn't go that far," Shakespeare said, wishing he could make the younger man understand. Many trappers despised Indians on general principles, and many Indians returned the favor for the same reason, or lack of it. He'd long speculated that if both sides could see the world through the eyes of those they hated, the constant bloodshed might stop, or at least taper off. The Shoshones and Flatheads were living proof that the red man and the white man could live together in harmony if they wanted. The pity was that so few cared to make the effort. "I'm only saying I understand it."

Nate saw Jenks open his mouth to argue and spoke up himself. "Let's keep going. I don't aim to sit here on this mountain all afternoon listening to the two of you squabble." Applying his heels, he moved out, following the prints. No rain had fallen in the interval since he'd sighted the war party, so the tracks were quite plain.

The younger man's attitude bothered Nate. There had been a time, back before Nate had ventured from New York City to the frontier, when Nate might have sympathized with Jenks's point of view. Since then he had learned that Indians and whites were more alike than either was willing to admit. And having lived with Shoshones for so long, he had learned to highly admire the Indian way of life. When someone branded them as evil, he took issue.

The Shoshones were friendly to all whites and always had been. Whenever a trapper visited a Shoshone village, he was made welcome with food and drink and a lodge to sleep in if he so desired. And the man need not fear for his belongings either. Unlike the Crows, who were addicted to petty thievery, the Shoshones were scrupulously honest in all their dealings.

Nate thought of them later that evening, after camp had been made and chunks of rabbit meat were roasting on the fire. "Did you happen to notice which direction the war party is heading?" he remarked.

"I did," Shakespeare said. "Toward Shoshone country."

"You'd think they'd be satisfied with Pointer's hair and my peltries," Jenks said bitterly.

"If these devils are Blackfeet," Pepin said, "they won't be content with anything less than a scalp for every one of them, and a new horse besides." He adjusted the stick suspended over the fire, turning the meat so the uncooked portions were nearest to the flames. "Maybe they're fixing to steal a few Shoshone women as well."

"Not the Blackfeet," Nate said. "They aren't much for taking wives from other tribes." He remembered a battle in which he had taken part some years back. "Men, women, children, it's all the same to them. The Blackfeet kill everyone."

"Like I said," Jenks mentioned smugly. "Savages, pure and simple."

The next day was a repeat of the first. About mid-morning Nate came to a creek where the war party had stopped to water their mounts. Not far beyond was a gravel bar the Indians had crossed. Mixed liberally with mud, the bar gave Nate a chance to study each and every set of hoofprints in detail. As he was doing so, he spotted a set of tracks much deeper than the rest. "This one was packing a heavy load. Maybe pelts."

"Could be," Shakespeare said, "although Jenks claims he had enough for two horses." He scratched his beard. "But where are all the other pack animals? What happened to all the supplies they stole? And Pointer's peltries?"

"Maybe we have the wrong band."

"Keep looking. We might find a clue."

Nate continued searching, and on a long muddy strip where the warriors had ridden strung out instead of in single file he found something odd. "I count eleven horses now."

"Me too," Shakespeare confirmed. "I thought I did back yonder and this proves it."

"Two more than I saw," Nate said thoughtfully. "This answers our question. I didn't see the whole band. There must have been more in the trees, and some of them are taking most of the plunder back to their village even as we speak."

"It's possible," Shakespeare conceded. "They wouldn't want to traipse all over the country with a lot of pack animals and provisions slowing them down."

"Especially if they're mainly after scalps," Nate said, pleased by the cleverness of their deduction.

That night they camped in a ravine sheltered from the blustery winds and enjoyed venison thanks to Pepin, who downed a small doe at 70 yards. Their horses were pushed to the limit the next day, and the next. Jenks's mount, normally used as a pack animal, was hard pressed to keep up the pace.

Nate was beginning to think it would be three or four days more before they caught their quarry when they had a stroke of luck. They discovered a spot where the war party had camped for two days, and the remains of an elk explained why.

"Soon now!" Pepin cried. "Soon we avenge our friend!"

It was the following day, early in the evening when the sun was slowly sinking behind a stark range of glistening peaks, that Nate came off a bluff and spotted in a basin below a pale pinpoint of light. Instantly he reined up and pointed. "There they are," he announced.

"At last," Jenks said. "I can't wait to get my hands on my furs."

"You'll have to wait a while longer," Shakespeare said. "We can't go barging on in there. First we scout out their camp, then we decide how best to kill them."

"I'll do the scouting," Nate said to forestall the others. He was concerned either the hotheaded Pepin or the brash Jenks might make a blunder that would prove costly to them all. Slanting into a stand of slender aspens, he climbed from the saddle, looped the reins to a limb, and started down the slope.

"Mind some company, son?" Shakespeare asked, falling into step.

"Not at all," Nate said gratefully.

A stretch of shrub and pines brought them to the basin floor, which was covered with high grass shaded greenish-gray by the gathering twilight. Halfway across the basin, at the base of a hillock dotted with trees, was the campfire.

"Cocky bunch," Shakespeare said. "Most war parties wouldn't bother with a fire this close to enemy territory."

"I've got three plews that says they're Blackfeet."

"You're on. I think they're Bloods."

Dropping low, Nate entered the grass and snaked forward. He loosened both flintlocks in case he needed them quickly, and slid his butcher knife partway out of its sheath once. The wind was on his back, a bad place for it to be since the war party's horses would pick up his scent if he wasn't extremely careful.

Three hundred yards were covered in virtual silence. Nate had learned the art of being stealthy from the Shoshones, some of whom were so adept they could sneak up on a bear and swat the beast on the rump before it knew they were there. He knew just how to lower his feet—toes first, with the weight born on the balls—to muffle the sound of his footsteps.

Low voices and laughter brought Nate up short. He guessed he was 20 to 30 yards from the fire, too close to dare rising for a look since his pale face would be a dead giveaway against the dark background. Easing onto his hands and knees, he crawled forward, glancing to the right where Shakespeare had been a few moments before. His friend was gone.

Nate wasn't worried. No other white man alive could handle himself like McNair, who would probably sneak so close to the camp he'd hear the warriors break wind. Nate, on the other hand, had no desire to push his luck; he crawled until he glimpsed the flames, then halted and contented himself for the time being with merely listening.

The tongue being used wasn't Blackfoot. Nate couldn't claim proficiency in the language, but the time he'd spent as a captive had given him an ear for recognizing it when he heard it spoken. Which narrowed the choices down to Piegans or Bloods, both allies of the Blackfeet in a fierce confederacy that controlled the northern Rockies and plains.

Presently, satisfied the band had no idea there was anyone else within 50 miles, Nate worked his way to the right, toward the hillock. He needed to know what sort of arms the warriors had, how many guns and bows and lances. At least one gun had been fired at Jenks, and they had to have at least one additional rifle and two pistols because that was how many guns Pointer had owned. Nate also wanted to learn where the horses were tied since he hadn't heard so much as a nicker out of them yet.

A faint rustling caused Nate to stop and look to his left. The rustling grew closer and closer. His gaze dropped, and so did his mouth when he distinguished the outline of a long, thin shape crawling directly towards him. *A snake!* he realized, instinctively tensing to draw back. Only he couldn't. He was closer to the camp, too close. The warriors might notice any sudden swaying of the grass.

The next moment the head of the reptile appeared, and Nate had to bite down on his lower lip to keep from crying out. Of all the types of snakes it could have been, this one turned out to be one of the deadliest of all: a rattlesnake.

Chapter Five

Even in the gloom of gathering night the distinct triangular shape of the rattler's head was plain to see. The markings on the scaly skin were harder to discern, not that they mattered. Nate knew that rattlesnakes did their hunting at night, knew that the one creeping slowly toward him was seeking prey, any warm-blooded prey it could find. He held himself rigid, hoping against hope the venomous reptile would simply pass him by. But such was not to happen.

When only a foot away from Nate's right hand, the rattler suddenly whipped its head high and coiled, its tiny forked tongue darting out to test the air. Its rattles shook, but not loudly.

Nate stared into the creature's unblinking eyes, into its bizarre vertical pupils, and felt his skin crawl with gooseflesh. The snake swayed, the tongue repeatedly flicking in and out. At such short range it could hardly miss if it chose to strike. Nate fought to resist an impulse to snatch his arm away since any movement would provoke the reptile into doing just that.

Nerve-racking seconds passed. Nate had no idea what the rattlesnake would do. Of all God's creatures, only grizzlies were as unpredictable. The Hawken was clutched in his left hand, of no use in swatting the snake aside even if he dared do so, since by the time he lifted the rifle the reptile would bite. All he could do was lie there and pray.

A full minute went by. Then, so lightning-quick its body was a virtual blur, the rattler whirled and sped off through the grass.

Nate exhaled in relief. His hands trembled slightly in reaction to his narrow escape. Waiting until he was composed, he resumed crawling around the base of the hillock, and once on the side opposite the camp he rose into a crouch. The wind had temporarily died, enabling him to hear the chirp of a cricket and the distant hoot of an owl. Even further off a lone coyote yipped its melancholy cry.

Holding the rifle in both hands, Nate advanced up the slope, wending around boulders, scrub thickets, and occasional pines. Three-fourths of the way to the top a log barred his path and he started to step over it. As his leg lowered, strong fingers abruptly clamped on his ankle. Thinking that an Indian had grabbed him, Nate elevated the Hawken to bash in the warrior's head. A barely audible chuckle stopped him.

"Getting a mite careless in your young age, Horatio. I heard you coming clear down at the bottom. Are you trying to get yourself killed?"

"You pick the darnedest times to play games," Nate whispered irately. His ankle was released, and he slipped over the log to squat beside his mentor. "Have you already spied on them?"

"Yep."

"Who won our wager?"

"See for yourself," Shakespeare said softly. Rising, he padded upward to the crest and lay down in a patch of cool grass.

Doing the same, Nate held his head low to the ground so the dancing firelight wouldn't reflect off him. Ten robust warriors were seated around the fire, all listening to one of their number who was going on at length about something. Nate noted the style of their hair and their buckskins and identified them as Piegans, which meant Shakespeare and he had both been wrong and neither of them had won their friendly bet.

Nate glanced to the right. At the base of the hill, shrouded in inky shadows, were the horses. He scanned the camp, spotting a number of bows and lances and a single fusee, but he saw no sign of the peltries and fixings stolen from Jenks and Pointer. He reasoned the goods were piled near the horses and couldn't be seen from his vantage point.

The Piegan doing the talking stopped, and another squared his shoulders and began speaking.

Nate had learned enough to know how best to spring the ambush. Easing backwards, he went a few feet before he pushed off the ground and hastened down the hillock. Shakespeare trailed him.

"Did you hear what they were saying?"

"You know I don't speak a lick of Piegan," Nate whispered.

"I've picked up a smattering of words," the mountain man said. "And if I'm right, they're fixing to attack a Shoshone village the day after tomorrow. They plan to steal a lot of horses and maybe count a few coup."

"Not if I can help it," Nate said. Now he had another reason for attacking the war party. The Shoshones were his adopted people, and he could not stand idly by while their enemies raided them.

Once on level ground the two trappers bore to the south and worked their way in a roundabout fashion to the aspens. They were at the edge of the trees when a clear metallic click stopped them in their tracks.

"*Non! Non!* It is our friends, young one."

"Yes, it's us," Nate confirmed, going on to find Pepin with a firm hand on the barrel of the greenhorn's rifle, which had been deflected downward. "Didn't it occur to you that it might be Shakespeare and me?" he asked Jenks.

"I wasn't thinking. I heard a sound and I assumed it might be Indians."

"That makes twice," Nate said, recalling the incident when Jenks had shot at them. "Keep it up and one of these times you'll make a mistake you'll live to regret."

"*Enfant!*" Pepin declared, and laughed.

Although Nate did not find the close call so amusing, he let the matter drop and turned to the issue at hand. "Here is what we found," he began. The Canadian and the youth were rapt listeners, and when Nate was done the Canadian smiled and slapped a thigh.

"Ten scalps to share! This is better than I dreamed."

"Our main purpose is to reclaim the stolen hides and such," Shakespeare mentioned.

"All I want is revenge," Jenks said eagerly.

"A dagger of the mind, a false creation, proceeding from the heat-oppressed brain," Shakespeare quoted.

"What?"

"Never mind," Shakespeare said, unwilling to waste words. There was nothing he could say or do that would change the young man's attitude, and rather than waste energy trying, he leaned against a sapling and crossed his arms. Some lessons could only be taught by life itself. Jenks would learn of his own accord, if he survived to learn at all.

Nate detailed the arrangement of the Piegan camp, concluding with: "They have no idea we're here, so if all goes well we can take them completely by surprise. I think we should sneak up on them from four directions and at a signal from me, open fire."

"I will take up position near their horses to keep any of the savages from getting away," Pepin said.

Nate suspected the *voyageur* had an ulterior motive. At the first blast of gunfire the Piegans would naturally dash for their horses to flee, enabling Pepin to drop more than he might otherwise, thereby giving him the chance to collect more scalps.

"What about me?" Jenks inquired. "I've never fought Indians before. What do I do?"

"You go to the top of the small hill," Nate suggested. The hillock, he figured, would be the safest place to be since it was highly unlikely any of the warriors would try to scale the slope while under attack. "If any of them go for the high ground, cut them off."

"I'll drop them like flies," Jenks pledged. "But where will you be?"

"Shakespeare and I will go through the grass, right up to their camp."

Jenks grinned. "Better you than me, King. If the Piegans spot you before you're ready, you'll be turned into pincushions."

"Thanks for the warning." Nate craned his neck to see up through the foliage. Every trapper learned early on how to tell the passage of time by the relative positions of the stars and the constellations, and by his reckoning it was then close to eight o'clock. "We'll wait until midnight to move out. By then most of them should be sound asleep."

"What do we do until then?" Jenks wondered.

"I don't know about you, but I aim to get some rest," Nate answered. Going over to a clear space amidst the saplings, he sat down with his back to a trunk, rested the Hawken across his legs, and tried to nap. The long day in the saddle had left him fatigued, but the impending clash had him too on edge to permit sleep. Shifting and squirming, he tried his best, until he heard a soft snicker.

"Ants in your britches, son?"

Nate looked around as McNair walked over and took a seat. "It's times like this I wish I had your knack for falling asleep anywhere, anytime."

"Blame Winona."

"You've lost me. What does she have to do with anything?"

"If your wife nagged you, you'd know how to drop off at the drop of a pin. No man likes to listen to a woman squawk at him from dawn to dusk, day in and day out. So men who find themselves in that situation learn to shut their wives out by falling asleep at will."

"And where did you pick up this tidbit of information? Your wife doesn't nag you either."

"No, she doesn't. But years ago I lived with another woman, a plucky Nez Percé, who just about wore my ears to a frazzle. I loved her too much to leave her, yet I couldn't take all that carping. Then one day she up and got herself taken by the Bloods during a raid, so I imagine some lucky Blood warrior has had to put up with her all these years." Shakespeare grinned. "There is justice in this old world, no matter what anyone says to the contrary."

"You're always full of surprises," Nate commented. His gaze drifted to the Piegan campfire. "Let's hope we're not in for any nasty ones when we make our move."

"You did right by having Jenks on the hill," Shakespeare said. "It'll keep him out of danger." His voice lowered.

Join the Western Book Club and GET 4 FREE* BOOKS NOW!
A $19.96 VALUE!

Yes! I want to subscribe to the Western Book Club.

Please send me my **4 FREE* BOOKS**. I have enclosed $2.00 for shipping/handling. Each month I'll receive the four newest Leisure Western selections to preview for 10 days. If I decide to keep them, I will pay the Special Members Only discounted price of just $3.36 each, a total of $13.44, plus $2.00 shipping/handling ($19.50 US in Canada). This is a **SAVINGS OF AT LEAST $6.00** off the bookstore price. There is no minimum number of books I must buy, and I may cancel the program at any time. In any case, the **4 FREE* BOOKS** are mine to keep.

*In Canada, add $5.00 shipping/handling per order for the first shipment. For all future shipments to Canada, the cost of membership is $16.25 US, which includes shipping and handling.
(All payments must be made in US dollars.)

NAME: _____

ADDRESS: _____

CITY: _____ **STATE:** _____

COUNTRY: _____ **ZIP:** _____

TELEPHONE: _____

E-MAIL: _____

SIGNATURE: _____

If under 18, Parent or Guardian must sign. Terms, prices, and conditions subject to change. Subscription subject to acceptance. Dorchester Publishing reserves the right to reject any order or cancel any subscription.

"Course, he's not the one who worries me."

"Pepin? He can handle himself."

"You'll get no argument there. But the man is too sure of himself. And he's got a powerful hankering for scalps. Worse case I ever saw. He would have been happier if he'd been born a Blackfoot."

"There you go again. Exaggerating as always."

"Think I do?" Shakespeare shrugged. "Well, let's hope so, for both our sakes."

For the next several hours Nate made small talk. He was too on edge to do anything else. Despite the many times he had engaged in mortal combat with enemies white and red alike, he could never get used to the idea. He wasn't one of those who liked to fight for the mere sake of fighting. If he had his druthers, he'd rather live in peace with everyone, but that was an impractical ideal, especially for one living in the untamed wilderness. Running into enemies, both human and bestial, was a common part of life in the mountains, and any man who wanted to last long had to accept that fact and live accordingly.

The crunch of a twig heralded Pepin. "It's about that time, my friends," he declared, pointing heavenward. "Are you ready?"

The location of the Big Dipper showed the Canadian was right. Nate stood, worked his legs to restore circulation, and checked the Hawken. None of them uttered a sound as he walked out of the trees and paused to regard the basin. "Spread out and stay low," he cautioned. "If you get into trouble, the rest of us will come to your aid."

"That's good to hear," Jenks said. His tone, his posture indicated his nerves were taut.

"Good luck," Nate offered. He touched Shakespeare's arm, then stalked forward as before. The light from the Piegan fire had dwindled to a few fingers of flame that would soon go out, which forced him to hurry in order to be in place before that happened.

Dread of encountering another rattler prompted Nate to stop every time he heard rustling. In each case it was the wind, which had intensified and was rippling the grass much as a gale rippled waves on the sea. Nate was halfway to the hillock when he thought to glance over his shoulder at the horizon and saw a mass of dark clouds blotting out many of the stars. A storm was coming. And if it got there before they were ready, it would spoil everything. In a driving downpour they wouldn't be able to see more than a few feet.

Disregarding caution, Nate hurried faster, parting the grass with his head and shoulders. He wondered if his companions had noticed the approaching storm and if they were doing as he was. Once his right hand came down on something wriggling and slippery, but there was no answering rattle and he plowed on ahead without bothering to find out what the thing had been.

The wind had an unforeseen effect. Nate was still 50 feet from the camp when the flames were smothered, plunging the immediate area into total darkness. Now Nate couldn't see where the Piegans were sleeping. Indeed, he had no idea whether a guard had been posted and where the warrior might be.

Frowning at the unwanted development, Nate moved steadily nearer. He didn't fear detection because the waving grass smothered any faint noises he made. About 20 feet out he sank onto his belly. Another ten feet brought him close enough to make out a few dark lumps on the ground by the fire. Sleeping Piegans, but he only counted five. Where were the rest?

Nate lifted his head to see better, then turned to ice on hearing a yawn off to the left. A slender figure was moving toward the fire, the lone man on watch, evidently. The Piegan knelt at the fire. Nate saw sparks blossom and promptly sank down. The guard was trying to get the fire going again.

Persistence paid off. After a dozen tries the brave rekindled the flames and held his hands out to shield them from the wind.

In the pale glow Nate saw the warrior's hawkish features. He now counted seven sleeping forms, which left two unaccounted for. The possibility of there being more than one guard was terribly worrisome. He scanned the hillock and the black shadows where the horses were tethered, but saw no one.

The Piegan, meanwhile, was feeding branches to the fire, raising the flames to new heights. He added too many, or maybe the wind flared the fire, but whichever was the case, the flames suddenly shot so high the Piegan had to leap back to keep from having his eyebrows singed.

At that moment a horse whinnied.

Instantly the Piegan was on his feet, and he wasn't the only one. Three others leaped up, bows in hand. They spoke in muted voices while gazing all around. Two of them then headed for the horses.

Nate was in a quandary. He wasn't sure if Shakespeare and Jenks were in position yet, and if he jumped the gun before they were ready, the whole element of surprise would be wasted. He watched with bated breath as the two warriors vanished in the murky shadows. The same or another horse nickered. There was a commotion but no outcries, no gunshots. He began to breathe a smidgen easier.

On the top of the hillock another commotion erupted. Someone cursed—in English. A tremendous crashing in the underbrush brought more of the sleeping Piegans to their feet in time to see a pair of men rolling down the slope, men who were locked together as each sought the other's throat. Rolling over and over and over, the combatants finally came to rest at the bottom.

Nate let out a gasp. Lester Jenks was grappling with a muscular brave, a brave who must have been on top of the hillock. A second sentry. The Piegans had not been as cocky as Shakespeare thought; they had taken prudent precautions against an attack.

Fierce yells broke out among the Piegans, and several moved to help their fellow. One drew a knife and coiled to plunge the blade into Jenks's back.

Something had to be done. Nate could wait no longer. Raising the Hawken, he took a hasty bead on the Piegan with the knife. But his thumb was in the act of curling back the hammer when another rifle cracked in the grass off to his left. Shakespeare's rifle it was, and the slug caught the knife-wielder squarely in the center of the back, ripping through the man's spine and bursting out his chest.

As the first Piegan fell, the rest whirled to confront the new threat. Nate shifted, sighted on a burly warrior, and gently squeezed the trigger. At the retort, the burly one was lifted from his feet and slammed lifeless to the ground.

The war party was in turmoil. They didn't know how many enemies they faced, and the deaths of two of their number in as many seconds had disconcerted the majority. Some broke, running for the horses. A few lifted bows, seeking targets to shoot. And a lone warrior turned back to assist the man grappling with Jenks. This warrior had a tomahawk, which he started to swing in an overhand arc.

Reloading the Hawken was out of the question. Nate drew his right flintlock, rising to one knee as he did. He snapped off a shot without aiming, and was gratified to see the ball strike the tomahawk-wielder in the armpit. The man jerked to one side, twisted, and fell.

Another pistol banged. Shakespeare had dropped a fourth warrior.

Barbed arrows sought the trappers.

Nate flattened again as a whizzing shaft streaked over his head, almost clipping his beaver hat. Yet another warrior dashed for the horses, leaving only two by the fire, one armed with a bow, the last holding a war club. Jenks was getting the worst of his fight; the Piegan was slowly choking the life from him.

Wedging the spent flintlock under his belt, Nate girded his legs, drew his other pistol, and surged forward, shooting as he straightened. The bowman, hit high in the chest, staggered and dropped his bow but did not fall. Nate unlimbered his tomahawk, uttered a Shoshone war whoop, and rushed to close quarters.

The Piegan bearing the war club charged to meet Nate. They clashed in front of the fire, the Piegan swinging first, a brutal blow that would have smashed Nate's skull to fragments had it landed. A swift parry with the tomahawk deflected it. Nate pivoted, slashing at the warrior's stomach. His foe, as nimbly as a chipmunk, danced aside.

Meanwhile, the wounded bowman had drawn a knife and was seeking an opening.

Nate was caught between the pair. He had to keep one eye on the man with the club, the other on the brave with the knife. Working in concert they might have downed Nate swiftly, but the wounded man was unable to do much more than stab ineffectively.

Suddenly Shakespeare McNair entered the fray, swinging his rifle as if it was a club, the stock crunching the wounded Piegan's nose and felling the warrior on the spot.

The warrior with the war club shrieked and made a frantic bid to cave in Nate's forehead. Nate countered, blocking the blow. In the process he hooked his right leg behind the Piegan's legs and shoved with his elbow, tripping his adversary. The Piegan landed on his back, got an elbow under him, and started to rise. Nate stopped him. Or rather, the keen edge of the tomahawk did by splitting the warrior's face right down the middle.

Nate wrenched the tomahawk loose and whirled to help Jenks. Aghast, he saw that he was too late. Lester Jenks lay limp in the grass, the hilt of a knife jutting from the youth's chest. There was no sign of the warrior who had killed him. "Where—?" he blurted out, glancing around.

Shakespeare was looking around also. "I think he ran for the horses," he said, and headed in that direction.

Nate immediately followed. There were still four Piegans unaccounted for. He'd expected to hear Pepin cut loose as warriors made for the string, yet there hadn't been a sound out of the Canadian, leading Nate to fear Pepin was dead too.

A body materialized in the night.

Both Shakespeare and Nate slowed. The corpse was that of a Piegan, his throat slit ear to ear. They went further and found another. A few yards more and there was a third, and bent over it, slicing off the scalp, was the grinning *voyageur*.

"*Magnifique!* Three scalps, all mine!" Pepin unbent and waved his grisly trophy in the air. "*Formidable*, eh, my friends? They never knew what hit them!"

Nate halted, breathing deeply as the swirl of violence caught up with him. His blood raged through his veins and he felt almost out of breath. He understood now why Pepin had not fired. The Canadian had not wanted to alert the fleeing Piegans to his presence, so he had dispatched them silently.

"Where's the last man?" Shakespeare asked, peering into the night.

"We missed one?" Pepin said. "That will not do. We cannot waste a scalp."

Coming as it did so soon on the heels of losing Jenks, Nate found the *voyageur*'s bloodthirstiness appalling. Turning, he walked toward their fallen friend. Behind him Pepin addressed McNair.

"Where is our young companion, *mon ami*?"

Nate did not hear Shakespeare's low response, but the Canadian's bellow of anger was like the bellow of a bull moose. Nate halted beside the dead greenhorn, sank to one knee, and took hold of the knife hilt to yank the weapon out. Jenks's eyes were wide open, staring blankly at the heavens. Nate let go of the knife to reach down and close the hapless trapper's eyelids, and as he did, rushing footsteps came at him from the right. He looked up just as the last of the Piegans, tomahawk in hand, screeched and sprang.

Chapter Six

Moments ago Nate King had tucked his own tomahawk under his belt. His hands were empty, his pistols also. But his left hand was near his knife. With the speed of thought he went to grab for it, then realized he could not possibly bring the knife into play before the Piegan slammed into him. So he brought both arms up, barely in time to cushion the impact as the heavy warrior bowled him clean over.

Nate landed flat, the Piegan astride his midsection. He tried to hurl the warrior from him, and the movement of his head as he lifted it saved his life because he moved it a hair to the left just as the brave's tomahawk cleaved the air, fanning his right ear. A punch to the Piegan's flat stomach elicited a grunt. The warrior, snarling, swept the tomahawk on high.

Getting his feet firmly on the ground, Nate bucked as a wild horse might, which threw the brave forward onto his shoulders. Nate was ready. Seizing the man's thighs as the Piegan slid upward, he heaved, throwing the warrior from him. In an instant Nate was in a crouch and clawing for his tomahawk.

The Piegan divined Nate's intent and aimed a blow at Nate's wrist, forcing Nate to pull his arm up or lose his hand. Nate scrambled backwards, trying to gain distance so he could employ a weapon, but the Piegan came after him, swinging constantly, a series of vicious swipes that would have ripped Nate to shreds if they had connected.

In the heat of personal combat a man's reflexes take over. If he tries to think, to reason out strategy, more often than not he loses his life during the precious seconds he is distracted by his own thoughts. Quite frequently inspiration saves the day, inspiration so elemental it stems from the most basic of instincts, the instinct for self-preservation.

Nate King had a strong sense of self-preservation. That instinct had carried him through dozens of conflicts with men and beasts alike. And it served him in good stead now. For as the Piegan delivered a particularly powerful blow that left the warrior momentarily off balance, Nate took a step toward the man instead of away from him and gouged his fingers into the Piegan's eyes.

Howling, the Piegan retreated a few feet, blinking furiously as his eyes filled with tears. He brushed his free hand over them, attempting to clear his vision.

In that crucial interval, Nate took the offensive. He leaped, grasped the warrior's wrist to keep the tomahawk at bay, and drove his other hand, fist clenched, into the Piegan's jaw. The warrior rocked on his heels. Nate punched again, and a third time, and suddenly the dazed Piegan crumpled, the tomahawk falling loose.

Nate pulled his knife and lifted it for the fatal stab. Helpless at his feet lay the Piegan, ripe for killing. Blade glinting in the firelight, the knife reached its apex, then froze there as Nate paused, his brow knitting. He wanted to bury the blade in the brave, but something stopped him, something stayed his hand at the very moment of making the kill. Whether it was the fact the Piegan was totally helpless or another factor, Nate didn't know. He just couldn't bring himself to finish the warrior off.

"Are you all right, son?"

Nate glanced up at Shakespeare and slowly nodded. "Fine," he said breathlessly. "Just a mite winded."

"Are you going to kill this rascal, or not?"

"No."

"Oh?" Shakespeare was perplexed, but they were such close friends that he offered no criticism or objections. Sliding his butcher knife out, he cut several strips from the Piegan's buckskin shirt and used them to securely bind the warrior's wrists.

A small boulder offered Nate a place to sit. He mechanically began reloading his pistols and commented, "Well, I guess that's that."

"We were lucky."

"Not lucky enough," Nate responded, looking at Jenks.

"What do you have in mind for this one?" Shakespeare asked, giving the Piegan a smack on the shoulder.

"I don't rightly know yet."

"I know what Pepin will want to do."

As if on cue, the fiery *voyageur* strolled up to them. Hanging from his belt were three fresh scalps, all dripping blood. He frowned down at Jenks, then glanced at the bound Piegan and looked startled. "What's this? You've spared one of the murdering bastards?"

"Yes," Nate said.

"How can you, after what they have done?" Pepin laid a hand on his knife. "Leave it to me, my friend. I will take care of this one for you, and to show you my generous nature, you can still have his hair."

"Don't touch him," Nate said.

Pepin paid no attention. "You're being foolish, and that's not like you." Grinning in anticipation, he leaned over the unconscious warrior and inched his knife from its sheath. "This will be all over in no time. A quick cut, and *voila*! It is done."

"*No!*" Nate practically roared, rising. "This one is mine, to do with as I see fit. Touch a hair on his head and so help me I'll put a ball into you."

"Into me?" Pepin said in amazement. "But we are friends, are we not? Surely you would not kill me to save one such as this?"

"I don't want him harmed," Nate reiterated.

"Most strange," Pepin said, stepping back and replacing his knife. "I do not understand but I will respect your wishes. Just remember this warning. You are making a mistake if you do not finish this man off here and now. A big mistake."

"I've made them before."

The Canadian glanced at McNair, who shrugged. "*Je ne comprends pas*," he muttered. "I will find the peltries and be right back." Shaking his head, he walked toward the horses.

Nate finished reloading one pistol and concentrated on the other. Without having to raise his head he knew that his mentor was staring at him, so he said, "Is something the matter?"

"Not with me."

"With me, you figure?"

"Alas, how is it with you?"

"Meaning?"

"Use every man after his desert and who shall escape whipping? Use them after your own honour and dignity: the less they deserve, the more merit is in your bounty," Shakespeare quoted, casting a meaningful look at the

Piegan. "In this instance, though, I have to agree with our impulsive friend from the North Country. You're making a mistake that could prove costly to you and yours. If you let this warrior go, he'll never rest until he's buried each and every one of us."

"He'd have to find us."

"Never put anything past fickle Fate."

Annoyed, Nate rose. "I have to fetch my Hawken." He entered the grass, following the trail of bent stems he had made to the spot where the rifle lay. Picking it up, he blew bits of grass and dirt off the barrel and the stock. Inwardly he was more upset with himself than the others because he knew in his soul they were right. To not slay the Piegan would be plain stupid, yet he balked at the notion and could not explain why. Was it because he was growing too softhearted for his own good? Was it because there had already been enough bloodshed, more than enough to make up for what the band had done to Pointer? Or was there some other reason altogether?

Shakespeare was examining the Piegan when Nate returned. "Uncanny, isn't it?" he remarked.

"What is?"

"How much this man resembles Drags the Rope. Why, they look enough alike to be twins."

Nate looked, and it was as if he saw the Piegan for the first time. He wondered why he had not noticed himself, and chalked it up to the heat of combat. Drags the Rope, after all, was one of his oldest friends, a Shoshone brave who had always treated him with the utmost respect and kindness. The two of them were like brothers, and there was nothing the one would not do for the other.

"Two peas in a pod," Shakespeare went on. He gave the warrior's left cheek a light slap, then did the same to the right. The Piegan's eyelids quivered but did not open, so

Shakespeare grabbed the man's chin and shook vigorously until they did.

Instantly the warrior tried to sit up. Shakespeare shoved him back down, and he snarled like a cornered beast and tugged in vain at the strips securing his wrists. When he discovered he was helpless he unleashed a string of furious words at his two captors.

"There's no need for me to translate," Shakespeare said. "Suffice it to say he has his dander up."

"Ask his name," Nate prompted.

Shakespeare spoke haltingly in the Piegan tongue, then relayed, "Black Badger. And he claims to have taken the scalps of seven whites."

"He's at our mercy and he tells you that?"

"No, he boasted of it."

The warrior went on at length with many angry glares at Nate and nods at his dead companions. On finishing he held his head high, proudly defiant.

"What was that all about?" Nate inquired.

"Black Badger wants you to know that one day he is going to cut open your stomach and rip out your entrails with his bare hands," Shakespeare reported. "He aims to make all of us suffer for our unprovoked attack, but you he hates the most. No one has ever bested him before. He thinks you must have a special charm given to you by your guardian spirit or else you are an evil spirit yourself."

"Tell him I'm just a man," Nate said, "and point out that we were justified in repaying them for what they did to Pointer and for stealing the hides they took."

Shakespeare passed on the information and listened intently to the Piegan's answer, his features troubled. "He claims he doesn't know what we're talking about. His war party hadn't set eyes on a single white man since leaving their village until we came along, and they didn't steal any pelts."

"Tell him we know better. Tell him that honest men don't speak with a forked tongue."

The warrior made a hissing sound on hearing the insult. His next words were barked out, clipped and precise.

"Black Badger says that your father was a Pawnee and your mother was a coyote. If he wasn't tied, he'd challenge you and let the Great Spirit show which one of you two has a straight tongue." Shakespeare paused and looked up. "I know an honest man when I meet one and this here is no liar."

"But what about the packhorse?" Nate mentioned. "War parties travel light and live off the land. Why did they bring an extra horse? What was on that one animal that made its hoofs sink so deep into the ground?"

The question was posed to the Piegan, who answered with bitter resentment.

"One of the warriors brought along a spare because his favorite war horse had just healed up after being wounded in a battle with the Sioux and the man wasn't sure if it would last the whole journey," Shakespeare disclosed.

"And the deep tracks?" Nate said.

"They shot an elk their fifth day out, and rather than let the meat go to waste, they packed as much as they could onto the extra horse and brought it along to eat along the way."

Nate was thoroughly confounded. The warrior's explanation made perfect sense, but he refused to believe it. If true, it meant that blaming the Piegans had been unjustified. It meant that tracking the war party down had been wasted effort. And it meant something far worse.

Pepin ambled toward them, a thumb hooked in his bright sash. "You will not believe this, my friends," he said. "I could not find the peltries anywhere. The savages must have cached their plunder along the trail and we will have to backtrack them to find it."

"Did you happen to see any elk meat lying around?" Shakespeare inquired softly.

"Was that what it was?" Pepin scrunched up his nose. "There's a lot of overripe meat wrapped in an elk hide over by the horses. Smells so awful a wolverine would pass it up!" He shook his head. "How they ate it is beyond me."

"Oh, Lord," Nate breathed, and had to sit down. His gaze fell on Jenks, on the youth's upturned, slowly stiffening face. The poor greenhorn had given his life needlessly. Nate felt a twinge of remorse, until he remembered that he had objected to going after the war party, that it had been Pepin and Jenks who'd insisted on the mission of vengeance. Had they listened to him, the youth would still be alive.

"What's wrong?" Pepin asked.

Nate told him.

"Can it really be?" the *voyageur* declared. "Well, *c'est la vie*! Mistakes happen sometimes, and there is nothing we can do about them except pick up the pieces and go on with our lives. *Oui?*"

"How can you—?" Nate began, and checked his anger before he made a statement they would both regret.

Shakespeare, touched by the turmoil he read in his friend's expression, commented, "Before any of us go around blaming anyone else, we all have to remember this worked out for the best."

"How do you figure?" Nate demanded.

"These Piegans were set to attack a Shoshone village. Think of all the lives we saved by stopping them before they could carry out the raid."

There was a point Nate had overlooked. They had indeed spared the Shoshones much death and misery, and he should be thankful he had been able to help his adopted people. His guilt started to evaporate. To take his mind off the affair completely, he worked at reloading the Hawken, but someone else wasn't content to let the matter drop.

"We must also remember, my friends, that Indians such as the Piegans live for war. Counting coup is everything to them, the measure of their manhood, their status in the tribe," Pepin stated. "When they ride off to attack their enemies they know full well they may never see their village again. We did no worse to them than any other tribe would have done."

Shakespeare nodded. "Honest plain words best pierce the ear of grief."

"What?" Pepin said.

"Old William S."

"When will you stop reading those silly plays and buy the works of a real man?" Pepin joked.

"Do you know of one?" Shakespeare asked drolly.

"What? You think Canadians can't read?" Pepin puffed up his chest. "Try the works of Rousseau. Or if you need your books in English, try Sir Walter Scott. Or Byron's masterpieces. Either knew more of life than your English bard."

Nate listened with half an ear to their exchange. It would have surprised many back in the States to learn that reading was a popular pastime for the trappers during the long, cold winter months when trapping was impossible. Books were freely traded back and forth, and in the course of four or five months a man might go through twice as many volumes. Not all the trappers indulged; some were content to lie abed with their Indian wives and not come out from under the blankets for days at a time.

Suddenly, while Pepin and Shakespeare were distracted by their conversation and Nate was busy with his rifle, the surviving Piegan leaped to his feet and bounded toward the end of the hillock with an agility and speed a black-tailed deer would have envied.

"Stop him!" Pepin bellowed. Suiting action to words, he lifted his rifle and took aim on the fleeing warrior's back.

"No!" Nate said, leaping up and pushing the barrel aside. "We take him alive."

"Not if we don't hurry," Shakespeare urged.

Whirling, Nate sped after the brave. He was upset with himself for not thinking to bind the Piegan's ankles as well as the wrists, and he wondered if perhaps, deep down, he secretly wanted the warrior to escape. A lone brave was no danger to the Shoshones. Once in the clear, the Piegan would no doubt head for home.

Black Badger glanced back, his face a study in determination. He came to the end of the hill and bore to the left, into the trees flanking it.

Nate was hard pressed to keep the warrior in sight. The thick brush, the quilt work of light and dark shadows, the low-hanging limbs, they all conspired to camouflage Black Badger, to render the man virtually invisible. Fortunately, the pumping motions of the brave's legs gave him away.

Nate also relied on his ears. The Piegan was making a lot of noise plowing through the undergrowth, cracking twigs underfoot and snapping off small branches. So whenever Nate temporarily lost sight of the brave, he only had to listen to know he was going in the right direction. For several minutes he tried hard to overtake the Piegan without success.

Then the noise stopped.

Nate ran another ten feet before he realized it. He halted, every nerve aquiver. About 40 or 50 feet to his rear Pepin was calling his name, but Nate wisely stayed quiet. Black Badger might be close by and Nate didn't want to give away his position. He crouched, breathed through his nose, and waited for the Piegan to resume the chase. But nothing happened.

Puzzled, Nate scoured every square inch of the foreboding forest. Other than the wind rustling the leaves, there was no sound. He figured Black Badger was lying low, waiting for him to give up and go back. The warrior was in for a surprise. Nate intended to stick on the trail.

Pepin fell silent. There was crashing in the undergrowth to the northeast which moved farther away with each passing second.

Still Nate didn't budge. He sensed that he was close to his quarry. A little patience, and he could march Black Badger back to the camp. And what then? Would he release the Piegan unharmed? If so, why bother going to all the trouble of hunting the man down?

Nate decided he was being outright foolish. He had no real wish to hurt the Piegan and no real desire to keep him a prisoner, so he might as well let the warrior go. Having made up his mind, he straightened and reversed direction, walking as he normally would, making no attempt to conceal the fact he was leaving so the Piegan would know it too. Ten yards he went, and then a slight noise behind him made him look over his shoulder.

A vague shape disappeared into a cluster of small pines.

Nate knew it was Black Badger. But what was the warrior doing following him? The brave should be in full flight elsewhere, making good his escape. Chuckling at the Piegan's stupidity, Nate went on. He hadn't gone more than five yards when his intuition blared and he spun around and saw a figure dive from sight in the undergrowth.

What a fool! Nate reflected, hiking northward. Had the situation been reversed, he would have been half a mile off already, not shadowing the very man he was trying to get away from.

The thought jarred Nate like a physical blow. There was only one reason the Piegan would be doing such a thing. *The hunter had become the hunted!* Again he stopped and spun, only this time there was no shadow to see. Of course not. The Piegan wouldn't make the same mistake a third time.

Raising the Hawken, Nate walked backward. He was the one who qualified as a fool for expecting the warrior to flee when Black Badger had clearly stated his intention to get revenge. Somehow, the warrior had slipped his wrists loose from the leather strips. Now the warrior was stalking him, biding time until a chance presented itself to close in.

Shouting for help would have been easy. Nate knew Shakespeare and the Canadian would swiftly come to his aid, but he couldn't bring himself to call their names. This was strictly between Black Badger and himself. He was the one who had fought the Piegan; he was the one who had spared the brave's life. If he had done as he should have done and slain Black Badger outright, he wouldn't be in the tight spot he was in.

The woodland took on a whole new aspect. Every shadow seemed sinister; every rustling leaf might be made by the man intending to take Nate's life. Nate looked right and left, trying to see everywhere at once. He cocked the Hawken, not caring if Black Badger heard the metallic click or not. Moving backwards as he was, he had to walk slowly, feeling his way so as not to trip over a root or a log. A single mistake would be all the Piegan needed.

Nate's right heel bumped something. Risking a look, he found a downed branch still bearing leaves. He lifted his leg high to step over, did likewise with the other leg, and kept retreating. Suddenly the vegetation on his left crackled.

Finger on the trigger, Nate pivoted, set to fire, and caught a glimpse of a rabbit leaping madly off. Any other time, he would have laughed at his jumpiness. Now, he grimly scanned the closest trees, his heart beating so loud he swore he could hear it.

Nate's heel scraped another object. This time it was a log as high as his knees. He had to twist in order to take a full stride, and as he did, during the instant when he took his eyes from the forest and was looking at the log, the night was rent by a bloodcurdling scream, a mixed whoop of feral hatred and rage. Nate tried to swing around, but he was standing sideways when a heavy body slammed into his right shoulder with all the force of a charging buffalo.

Chapter Seven

Nate King was borne backwards as iron arms banded around his own, preventing him from using the Hawken in any way or from grabbing for a pistol. His lower legs smashed into the log, which sent him tumbling hard onto his shoulders on the other side. The contorted features of Black Badger were inches from his own, the gleam of intense hatred in the Piegan's glittering eyes giving him the aspect of an enraged demon.

At the instant of slamming onto the ground, Nate's finger involuntarily tightened on the trigger and the rifle went off, booming loud in his ears. The ball thudded into the ground. Nate tried to ram the barrel against the warrior's head, but was unable to raise his arms high enough. A knee gouged into his groin, flooding him with agony. In order to defend himself he let go of the rifle, and the two of them commenced rolling back and forth as each sought to get a grip on the other's throat.

Black Badger succeeded. Nate winced as fingernails bit into his skin, digging deep into his flesh. He gripped the brave's wrists and pulled, but he might as well have been pulling on the wrists of a bronze statue. Black Badger seemed endowed with inhuman strength. Stark hatred, it was said, could do that.

Nate tried flipping the Piegan off, but it was like trying to flip a slippery eel. Black Badger knew just how to twist and shift to frustrate every attempt Nate made. And all the while his bony fingers dug ever deeper into Nate's neck, cutting off Nate's wind.

In the distance there were yells. Shakespeare and Pepin were on their way, but Nate knew they would arrive too late to be of any help. Only he could preserve his life. To do that, he abruptly stopped pulling on Black Badger's arms and swooped a hand to his butcher knife.

Black Badger must have felt the movement, for he released his hold and clutched at Nate's wrist just as the knife leaped free of its beaded sheath. Nate angled his arm to stab and was thwarted by his foe. Straining with all their might, they struggled for an advantage: Nate to break loose so he could use the knife, Black Badger to wrench Nate's arm hard enough to compel Nate to drop the weapon.

A boulder settled the issue for them. They rolled against it, and Nate nearly cried out when his forearm smashed into the obstacle and the knife was knocked from his grasp. Thinking fast, he drew his tomahawk. Equally fast, Black Badger seized his left wrist.

Again they tussled. Nate wound up on top. He managed to tear his arm free and whipped the tomahawk overhead for a killing stroke. Black Badger lashed out with both legs, his heels lancing into Nate's midsection. Nate was hurled backward, tripped, and fell. By the time he scrambled to a knee, the Piegan was on him again.

Both of Nate's wrists were snatched and held as he was propelled rearward into a tree trunk. Nate put every ounce of energy he had into pushing the warrior from him, yet it wasn't enough. It appeared he had finally met his match; more than his match.

Those were awful moments. Nate was nose to nose with a crazed fiend who thirsted for his blood, and he was powerless to keep the man at bay. He tried hooking a leg behind the Piegan and shoving, but Black Badger was too crafty for him. He tried ramming a knee into the warrior's groin, but Black Badger avoided the blow. Nothing Nate did worked.

Then, unbidden, a memory flashed through Nate's mind, a memory of a talk he'd had with Shakespeare some years ago, shortly after the pair met. They had been discussing hostiles, and Shakespeare had said, "As sure as you're breathing, there will be times when you find yourself going at it tooth and nail with some brave who fancies your scalp. When those times come, remember this: Anything goes in a fight. There are no rules. There's no right or wrong way to save your hide. Do whatever the hell you have to in order to survive. Biting, scratching, kicking, you name it. Whatever it takes."

Those words were like soothing ointment on a burning wound. Nate remembered them as if they had been spoken the day before, and with the memory came action. Closing his eyes, he drew his head back, then brought his forehead crashing down onto the Piegan's nose. Cartilage crunched. Blood gushed. The warrior's grip weakened and Nate immediately shoved, throwing the brave from him. Black Badger stumbled but didn't fall.

Nate stepped to the left, gaining room to move, drawing both pistols and cocking them as he did. Black Badger wiped a forearm across his eyes, snarled, and sprang. "Not this time," Nate said, firing the right flintlock. The ball cored the warrior's chest, spinning Black Badger completely around. The Piegan looked down at himself, blinked once, then unexpectedly pounced, his arm upraised, his lips curled in fury. Nate shot again, the left flintlock this time, and a hole appeared in the center of Black Badger's brow. Carried along by its own momentum, the body toppled toward Nate, who nimbly darted out of the way. The thud of the warrior hitting the earth signified the end of the clash.

Nate was suddenly very tired. He walked to the log and sat down, his arms hanging. Through the brush came a pair of buckskin-clad figures who drew up short on spying him and the corpse. No one spoke for a bit.

Shakespeare lowered his Hawken and came forward. "You okay, son?"

"Never better."

"Hurt anywhere?"

"Not a scratch."

"You don't sound so good."

Sighing, Nate wagged a pistol at the Piegan. "I tried to do the right thing and look at what happened. I nearly got myself killed."

"No one ever claimed doing right would be easy. Sometimes our head tells us it's one way while our heart tells us it's another. Choosing is where wisdom comes in."

Pepin chuckled and swaggered to the dead Piegan. "Lord, McNair! Sometimes you're worse than a Bible-thumper. King has no cause to be upset. He did what he had to do." Pepin nudged Black Badger with his toe. "He just should have done it sooner and spared himself a lot of trouble."

"Is it really that simple?" Nate asked.

"It is to me, *mon ami*," Pepin said. "It's useless to fret yourself sick over killing an enemy. *Certainment*, no one in their right mind ever wants to take another life, but if it has to be done, if you have no choice, then do the killing and forget about it and you'll be better off. That is my outlook."

Nate slowly stood, and went about collecting his scattered weapons. He had to search long and hard for the butcher knife, which lay hidden in thick grass. Then he reloaded his guns. His friends waited patiently, both well aware that it was unwise for a trapper to go anywhere unarmed. As they made their way toward the hillock, Nate asked, "What now?"

"What else? We go dig up our cache and head back," Pepin said. "I don't know about you, but I can hardly wait to see my woman again. She'll have missed me so much, I don't think we'll come out of the lodge for a week."

"The Nez Percé have their villages along the Snake at this time of year, don't they?" Shakespeare commented.

Pepin nodded. "That's where I'll find my sweet *femme*."

"What about Jenks?" Nate brought up.

"What about him?" the *voyageur* responded.

"What are we going to do with his belongings?"

"We divide them up between us."

"That wouldn't be right."

"*Mon Dieu!* Here you go again."

"Jenks has kin back in the States," Nate reminded the Canadian. "I say we sell his stuff for whatever it will bring at the upcoming Rendezvous and send the money back with the supply train to St. Louis. Someone can relay the funds to his family from there."

"What a waste," Pepin lamented. "We won't get more than fifty dollars for his rifle and possibles."

Fifty or ten makes no difference."

"You are a hard man, Grizzly Killer," Pepin said, and cracked a grin. "But yes, we will do what is right by our former partner. Our consciences will be clean." He clapped

Nate on the shoulder. "Being around you is having a bad influence on me. At this rate, you'll have me giving up drinking and women before I know it." He glanced around. "But what about the Piegan mounts? Surely we're not selling them too? Can't we split them up among us?"

There was no reason not to, and Nate remarked as much.

"Good. There is hope for you yet."

The storm struck shortly after they buried Lester Jenks. Nate had already gone after their own animals, so they moved all the horses into the shelter of the forest. A lean-to was erected to protect them from the elements, and while lightning blazed and thunder rumbled, they sat snug and dry in front of a tiny fire, each man lost in his own thoughts.

Dawn broke crisp and clear. They were in the saddle before the sun had completely risen, wending their way northward. With so many horses to manage, they were spaced out over 40 yards or better. Pepin had the lead, Shakespeare was halfway back, and Nate brought up the rear with the four horses under his care.

The next day the same arrangement prevailed. As usual, wildlife was everywhere, and Nate lost himself in the wonders of the mountain paradise he'd chosen to call home. He never tired of studying wild creatures; they were a constant source of entertainment and instruction. Tiny scampering chipmunks or huge grazing elk, they all fascinated him equally.

On the third day, as they were crossing a luxuriant valley, Nate glanced to his right at hills bordering the grassy flatland and spotted a splash of red among the pines. Curious, he reined up. The shape of the red object was circular and didn't appear to be moving. Since Nature never painted her handiwork such a bright crimson hue, it had to be something man-made.

"What's the matter?" Shakespeare called.

"Come have a look-see," Nate answered.

Pepin rode back also. "A flower, you think?" he said when he saw the red dot.

"Too big," Nate replied.

"A marker of some kind, then?"

"There's only one way to find out." Nate gave his lead rope to Shakespeare. "Watch my horses don't run off."

"You be careful," McNair cautioned. "It might be a Blackfoot trick. Once I saw a band fly an American flag so unsuspecting trappers would walk right into their camp, thinking they were friendly. A few dunderheads did too. They lost their hair so fast, they didn't have time to blink."

Resting the stock of the Hawken on his thigh, Nate galloped to the bottom of the hill. From there the red object was difficult to see, screened as it was by a thicket and pines. Dismounting, he ground-hitched the black stallion so he could ride off swiftly if he had to.

On panther's feet Nate padded upward, always staying low to the ground to minimize the target he presented. He caught glimpses of the red object now and then, but not enough of a glimpse to tell him what it was. At length he squeezed through a thicket, and lying in an open patch of ground was what had drawn his interest: a red woolen cap, similar to Pepin's.

Perplexed, Nate picked up the cap to inspect it and found dark stains made by dried blood. A lot of blood. Looking down, he saw red splotches dotting the earth, leading off into a bunch of spruce trees. Leveling the Hawken, he followed the dots.

In the valley below, the *voyageur* turned to McNair and asked, "What the hell is he doing? If he goes into those trees we will not be able to see him at all."

The same thought had occurred to Shakespeare, and he did not like it one bit. "I taught him better than that," he grumbled. Lashing his reins, he made for the hill. "Come on. We might as well stay close in case he gets into a fix again."

"*Oui*. He does have a flair, does he not?"

"In faith, he is a worthy gentleman, exceedingly well read, and profited in strange concealments, valiant as a lion, and wondrous affable, and as bountiful as mines of India."

"Are we talking about the same man?"

"Lord, Pepin. You're a regular barbarian."

"And loving every minute of my barbaric life."

Shakespeare observed Nate disappear in the spruce stand and cursed under his breath. The younger man took too many needless risks. He rode faster, leaped from the saddle before his white horse fully stopped, and was off up the hill like a spry mountain goat. Since haste was called for, he didn't try to move silently. Behind him came Pepin.

A faintly bluish tinge set the spruce trees apart from other nearby pines. They formed nearly even rows, an impenetrable phalanx to the unaided eye. Shakespeare saw Nate's footprints next to a trail of blood, divined why Nate had gone into the stand, and advanced with his senses primed.

In the center the pines widened. There, prone in a patch of grass, lay the mutilated body of a trapper. Beside it squatted Nate, who looked up and frowned. "Another one," he said grimly. "Just like Pointer."

The similarities were obvious. Like Harold Pointer, this man had been stripped, his abdomen sliced wide, and his intestines strewn about. His neck had been severed. Additional atrocities had rendered the body as ghastly in every respect as Pointer's.

"The Piegans, you figure?" Pepin speculated.

"You know better," Nate said. "This was done within the past twenty-four hours. Look." He pointed. "The ravens haven't even gotten to the eyes yet."

"Then who?" Pepin said, stepping forward. He saw the cap in Nate's hand, stiffened, and grabbed it. "Can it be? This is the cap of a *voyageur*! But who?" Leaning down, he took hold of the dead man's shoulder and slowly flipped the body over. On seeing the man's face clearly, he exhaled loudly and clapped a hand to his brow. "*Qu'est-ce que c'est?* Labeau! What a terrible end, my old friend!"

"You know him?" Shakespeare said.

"Yes. Some years ago in Canada. We worked for the same company for a while, then went our separate ways. I'd heard that he ventured south, but I had no idea he was in this territory."

Nate lowered a finger close to bruise marks on the trapper's wrist. "It looks like some of them held him down while someone else did the carving."

"The bastards!" Pepin declared. "Wherever these murderers are, they must pay for their crimes! This vile act must not go unpunished."

"Here we go again," Shakespeare muttered.

The grass had been torn up by the struggle. Nate studied the various tracks, and discovered where a half-dozen men had headed east out of the spruce stand. He stuck to their path, which brought him, minutes later, to a clearing where horses had waited, 18 or 19 in all. Most of the hoofprints dug deeply into the soil, as they would if the animals were heavily burdened. He was scrutinizing them when a low voice to his rear made him jump.

"We owe it to the Piegans, if not ourselves."

Nate locked his eyes on Shakespeare's. "Oh, we owe it to ourselves, all right. They're not more than a day ahead of us, and with all the pack animals they have, they won't make very good time."

"There are seven of them."

"There were nine Piegans and that didn't stop us."

"But these aren't Indians, and you know it."

"Yes," Nate admitted. The idea had been growing ever since Jenks described eluding the men who stole his hides. Jenks had been a greenhorn, as inexperienced as a newborn baby; he'd known next to nothing about wilderness lore, hadn't the vaguest idea how to hide his tracks. Any self-respecting Indian would have hunted Jenks down with ease. And no war party would have given up the search for Jenks so readily, not when one of their number stood to gain a fresh scalp, which warriors prized above all else. No, now that he thought about it in depth, he fully realized that the band responsible for slaying Pointer and taking Jenks's belongings had to have been a band of white man. "But who would do such a thing?" he wondered aloud.

"Cutthroats of one sort or another," Shakespeare said. "Men who value the price they can get for a stolen pelt more than they do the value of a human life." He scoured the clearing. "Who knows how many innocent trappers they've killed?"

Nate stiffened as a recollection came to him. "Do you remember the last Rendezvous?"

"How could I forget it? My wife bought so much it about left me broke."

"This is serious," Nate said. "Do you remember that talk we had with Bridger and Meek one night?"

The light of understanding brightened Shakespeare's eyes. "Sure do. Bridger told us that it seemed the Blackfeet were a lot more active of late than they used to be. Meek said that by his calculations there were close to twenty trappers who didn't show up for the Rendezvous who were supposed to."

"Twenty," Nate repeated, the full implications appalling him. "And everyone just naturally figured the Blackfeet were to blame."

"There might be a lot more we don't know about," Shakespeare said, "since we have no way of telling how many seasons this bunch has been going about their vile business."

"Whoever cooked this scheme up is no idiot," Nate said.

Shakespeare nodded. "They must concentrate on a small region at a time and murder every trapper they can find, making it look as if Indians are to blame. Then they clear on out and no one is the wiser."

"We fell for their trick," Nate said bitterly. "We were all too eager to pin the blame on the Piegans."

"Now we know better."

"Whoever these vermin are, we have to hunt them down and put an end to them before any more trappers lose their lives," Nate declared.

Shakespeare, in the act of moving around the clearing, paused, his brow knitting. "There's something else about that last Rendezvous. Everyone was talking about a certain trapper who'd supposedly caught more beaver in one year than anyone else ever had. He even beat out Jed Smith."

"I heard the same story," Nate confirmed. "But I can't recall his name." He pondered a bit. "All I remember is that he brought in over eight hundred peltries." Something else came to mind. "And there were a few others who had good years too. Real good years. I'll bet they're the ones we want."

"Don't jump to conclusions," Shakespeare cautioned. "Some of them might have been legitimate. We won't know who to hold accountable until we catch this outfit."

"And catch them we will, *mon ami*!"

Both Nate and Shakespeare turned at the angry bellow and saw Pepin striding toward them, Labeau's cap still clutched in his brawny hand.

"I heard some of what you just said," Pepin informed them, "and I have never been so mad in my life!" He gave the cap a furious shake, as if throttling a throat. "The ones who butchered poor Labeau will not live long enough to butcher anyone else. This I vow!"

"We're in this together," Shakespeare said, "and we can't go rushing off half-cocked. We have to be mighty careful. The men we're after are utterly ruthless."

"So?" Pepin touched his knife. "I can be just as ruthless when the need arises." He spat, then wiped a sleeve across his mouth. "Just thinking of these sons of bitches puts a rotten taste in my mouth. We must go after them and stay on their trail until we catch up, no matter how long it takes us."

"What about all the extra horses we have?" Nate mentioned. "They'll slow us down."

"We'll have to let them loose in a meadow and hope they're still there when we get back," Pepin proposed.

Shakespeare walked over. "I have a better idea. We can do like the Comanches do when they hunt wild horses."

"The Comanches?" Pepin said. "They are the Indians who live far down in the Red River country, are they not? I do not know much about them."

"All you need to know is how they hunt mustangs." Shakespeare grinned as he went into detail. "Several warriors will go out together, each with a string of two or three mounts. When they spot a wild herd, they give chase, and as each one of their mounts tire, they change to another horse without their feet so much as touching the ground."

"I get it," Nate said, excited by the possibilities. "They run the wild herd into the ground and then catch whichever ones they want."

"Exactly," Shakespeare said. "There's no reason we can't do the same thing. With all the horses we have, we should overtake these butchers in a third of the time it would ordinarily take us."

"Très intelligent!" Pepin exclaimed. "Why did I never think of that?" He held out his hand, palm downward, and said, "Now we make the pledge."

Nate looked at him. "Pledge?"

"Oui. Put your hand on mine and I will commit us to our noble cause."

Feeling somewhat sheepish, Nate obeyed the *voyageur.* Shakespeare added his hand, his expression grave.

Pepin gazed skyward and cleared his throat. "We solemnly pledge to track these fiends to the ends of the earth, so help us God! And if we fail, may maggots eat our innards and worms crawl in our ears!" Pleased, he smiled at each of them and nodded. "Now we are committed."

Together they headed down the hill. Nate, bringing up the rear, couldn't shake the mental picture of maggots squirming in his entrails, which he sincerely hoped wasn't a harbinger of things to come.

Chapter Eight

For the rest of that day the three trappers put the Comanche system to the test, and found it worked extremely well. Where possible, they held their horses to a steady trot, and when an animal flagged they simply switched to another and added the tired horse to their individual strings. In this way they covered twice as much ground as they ordinarily would have, and by sunset they were many miles from the hill where Labeau lay in a shallow grave, and at a much lower elevation.

Camp was made in a gully where they could build a small fire without fear of it being seen from afar. Supper consisted of jerky and water. Afterward, they turned in so as to be able to get an early start the next day.

Sunrise found them already on the trail. The killers had tried to hide their tracks, but with so many pack animals in tow, they had wasted their energy. Even on the rockiest ground there were plenty of chips and scratch marks to guide the three trappers.

Toward the middle of the day, as they came to a narrow valley, Shakespeare, who was in the lead, suddenly drew rein and gestured. "Smoke," he announced.

Two miles distant a tendril of gray was rising to meet a puffy white cloud.

"It's them!" Pepin cried. "Now we make good on our pledge! Soon the ground will run red with their blood!" Working his legs, he began to swing his horse past McNair's string so he would be the one in front.

"Hold on," Nate said. "Charging on in there would only get us all killed. We'll take it nice and easy, just as if we were up against hostiles."

"Bah!" Pepin waved his rifle at the smoke. "I say we ride in with our guns blasting and cut them down before they can so much as lift a finger against us."

Shakespeare leaned on his saddle horn and grinned. "There isn't much that amazes a man my age. When you've seen and done practically everything, surprises are few and far between. But Pepin, you fit the bill."

"How so?"

"I don't know how in the world you've lived as long as you have," Shakespeare said. "As impetuous as you are, you should have gone under by the time you were ten." He lifted his reins and his horse moved out. "Since Nate and I aren't partial to the notion of pushing up buffalo grass, you'll do as we say and go about this slow and careful."

A few mumbled words were Pepin's only comment.

Another mile fell behind them. Shakespeare slanted northward, sticking to thick cover but never losing sight of the smoke. When within half a mile of the camp, he drew rein, dismounted, and secured his horses to a cottonwood. "One of us has to go on ahead for a look-see."

"Me," Nate said.

"Not this time," Shakespeare replied, hurrying into the

woods before anyone could stop him. He heard Nate curse, and chuckled. The younger man's concern was touching, but Shakespeare didn't need anyone mothering him and felt that it was high time Nate realized the fact.

Holding his Hawken in his left hand, Shakespeare stealthily crept closer and closer to the few wisps of smoke still hovering in the air. The fire, evidently, was going out. He was puzzled as to why the band had stopped so early, but was glad they had. The sooner the whole gory business was done with, the happier Shakespeare would be.

The acrid scent of burning wood brought Shakespeare to a stop behind a pine. Peering out, he spied several tiny flickering flames at the edge of the forest, where the grassy valley floor began. Oddly enough, he saw no one, nor any horses.

Bending low, Shakespeare advanced cautiously. The area around the fire was completely deserted, causing him to conclude the band had already gone on. Prudently, he didn't show himself until he was at the very last tree and had verified it was indeed safe to step into the open.

Tracks were everywhere, both the footprints of the cutthroats and the hoofprints of their many horses. Shakespeare walked to the fire, then gazed out across the valley. The band had no more than an hour start, he deduced. "We'll get you soon," he said softly, and was about to leave when his eyes fell on moist drops of blood.

Shakespeare touched a fingertip to the largest drop. Having skinned so many beaver and other animals over the years, he knew exactly how fast blood dried. The sticky consistency of the drops indicated they had been made within the past two hours. A trail of them led into the high grass.

"Not again," Shakespeare said to himself. Cocking the

rifle, he followed the trail, noticing how the drops grew bigger and bigger the farther he went. About 30 feet out he saw the body, lying face down. Unlike the other victims, this one was fully clothed. "Damn!"

Shakespeare knelt, set the Hawken down, and gripped the man's shoulders to roll him over. Suddenly a hand darted out, a bloody hand grasping a gleaming dagger, the blade spearing at Shakespeare's throat. Shakespeare jerked his head to the right and felt the man's sleeve brush his neck. He grabbed the arm, then held fast. "Hold on there! I'm a friend."

"McNair?" A bearded, lined face, seamed with pain, gaped up at him. "Is it really you?"

"Nelson?" Shakespeare released the arm and quickly rolled the man onto his back. "Tim Nelson?"

"Help me, please."

Shakespeare was already lifting the trapper to carry him to the fire. He'd met Nelson at a Rendezvous four years ago, and on several occasions since they had played cards and shared drinks. "Hold on. We'll do what we can to patch you up."

"Help—" Nelson said, his voice fading as his eyelids fluttered and trembled as if having a fit. Gasping loudly, he passed out.

A rare rage seized Shakespeare McNair as he hastened out of the high grass and gently deposited Nelson close to the fire. He drew a pistol, pointed it at the ground, and banged off a shot as a signal to his friends. Then he bent down.

The cutthroats had done a thorough job. Blood seeped from bullet holes in both ankles and both knees. The left shoulder, broken by a ball, was bent at an unnatural angle. And as if those wounds weren't enough, someone had stabbed Nelson three times low in the back.

Shakespeare marveled that the man was still alive. Depending on how severe the stab wounds were, Nelson might survive provided he had a lot of doctoring. That in mind, Shakespeare rekindled the fire and had the flames crackling when his companions showed. "We need hot water," he announced.

Nate was first off his horse. He stared, then commented, "I know him from somewhere."

"That you do," Shakespeare established, and quickly explained, finishing with, "If we can stop the bleeding, maybe he'll pull through."

Pepin was standing a few yards away, his arms folded across his chest. "Why go to all the bother?" he asked. "It might be a waste of our time, and those we are after will get farther and farther away."

"I can't believe you can be so cold-blooded," Shakespeare snapped. "So what if they gain a little lead on us? This is a fellow trapper we're talking about."

"Is it?" Pepin said. "I wonder."

"What the devil do you mean?"

"How do we know he isn't one of *them*? How do we know he didn't have a falling out with the others and they left him for the vultures, no?"

The idea had not even occurred to Shakespeare. He studied Nelson's face while reflecting that he actually knew very little about the man. And now that he thought about it, he hadn't seen Nelson for a year or better. What had the man been up to in all that time?

While the grizzled mountain man pondered, Nate was searching for water. It stood to reason that no one would make camp where water was unavailable, so he was certain there must be some within short walking distance of the fire. Since there was no stream anywhere in sight along the valley floor, he concentrated on the forest behind the camp and located a small spring. There, as he knelt to fill the coffeepot, he noticed a small footprint in the soft mud at the water's edge. The size was such that it had either been made by an extremely small man or a woman. Assuming a man had to have been responsible, he thought no more about the track as he hastened the filled pot back to heat it over the rekindled fire.

Nate told Pepin about the spring, and the *voyageur* took the horses to drink. Then Nate turned to his mentor. "What do you think? Could Pepin be right?"

"Nelson always struck me as the honest sort, but honest men go bad on occasion. I don't know," Shakespeare admitted. "It would explain why he's the only one we've found who wasn't stripped and hacked apart."

Shakespeare drew his knife and leaned over Nelson's left leg. Nate did likewise with the right. Together they carefully cut the buckskin leggings open to fully expose Nelson's severely swollen ankles and knees. They did the same with the shoulder wound.

"We'll have to set this broken bone soon," Shakespeare mentioned. "It'll hurt like hell. I hope he doesn't come around until after."

But Nelson revived as they were dabbing hot water on his ankles. Groaning, he sluggishly tried to lift his head but couldn't.

"You lie still, Tim," Shakespeare said. "Save your energy for later."

"Can't," Nelson said weakly.

"Mister, you do as we tell you," Nate advised. "We'll do our best to pull you through, but you have to help."

"Forget about me," Nelson said. "This coon is a goner."

"Nonsense," Shakespeare responded.

"You saw where I was stabbed," Nelson said, and winced. "I'm bleeding inside. I can feel it." He coughed once. "The knife Belker uses is over a foot long."

"Belker?" Nate said.

"One of those riding with Galt." Nelson coughed some more, and when the fit subsided there was a drop of blood at the corner of his mouth.

Nate and Shakespeare exchanged knowing looks.

"Forget about me," Nelson reiterated. "Save her."

"Who?" Shakespeare asked.

"Clay Basket, my woman. They took her, the scum!" Nelson flushed with outrage and the drop of blood became a trickle. "She fought them as best she could, kicking and clawing like a wildcat, but they tied her to a horse as if she was some animal and rode off with her. They all laughed at me too as they went by, laughed and bragged of how they're fixing to treat her." He tried to raise a hand to seize Shakespeare's wrist, but couldn't. "She won't last two days in their clutches. Promise me you'll go after her, McNair! Promise me you'll get her safely to her people, the Crows!"

"Calm down," Shakespeare said. "We'll do what we can for her just as soon as we tend to you."

"*No!*" Nelson cried. "Haven't you been listening to a word I've said? I'm not important. She's the one you have to help." His skin turning ashen, he tried to push up on his elbows.

"You're making yourself worse," Nate said, putting his hands on the man's chest and pressing. "Just lie quietly."

"I don't care about me! Save her, damn it!" Nelson glanced from one of them to the other. "Haven't either of you ever had a wife? Haven't either of you ever been in love? Clay Basket is everything to me! Don't let those bastards have their way with her."

"We'll head out in a bit," Nate said, touching the wet strip of buckskin he held to the blood on Nelson's chin.

"Fill us in, Tim," Shakespeare coaxed. "We need to know who we're up against."

Nelson gave a curt nod, then closed his eyes. "They showed up about sunset yesterday, just as we were sitting down to supper. Acted real friendly at first. They hailed us, then rode on in with their hands empty to show they meant us no harm. When I found they were white, the first white men I'd laid eyes on in over a year, I was glad for the chance to chaw and catch up on the latest news."

"You've been living with Clay Basket's people?" Nate guessed.

"Yep. They took me in when I was about froze to death, and half starved to boot. Clay Basket herself doctored me." Nelson's voice acquired a wistful quality. "I've never known a woman like her. So kind, so caring. She brought me back from the dead, and ever since I've been with her village, helping hunt and fight off the Blackfeet and such." He stopped, took a lingering breath, then continued. "About a month ago I got the fool notion of taking up trapping again. I'd lost all my fixings, but I figured I could find someone to stake me at the next Rendezvous."

Nate saw that the man was weakening fast. "About the men who did this to you? About Galt and Belker?"

"There are seven of them. Galt is the brains of the bunch," Nelson said. "When they first rode in, I couldn't believe how many peltries they had. Eleven horses piled high as could be! They claimed they'd had a run of luck and like a jackass I believed them."

"When did they turn on you?"

"This morning. We had just finished up breakfast when Galt grinned at me, said he'd taken a liking to my woman, and wanted to know if I'd be partial to selling her.

When I told him she was my wife and I wouldn't give her up for all the furs they had, Galt laughed and said he'd just have to take her." A low moan escaped Nelson's lips. "I wouldn't let any man talk that way to me, so I jumped up and was set to bash his face in when all the rest of them pounced on me and pinned me down. Clay Basket tried to help but one of them wouldn't let her."

"You don't have to go on," Nate said.

"I want to." Nelson opened his eyes. "They taunted me, called me an Indian-lover. Galt bragged of how he and his friends are growing rich by robbing every trapper they can find. They were going to let me live when they learned I didn't have any pelts, but then Galt took a fancy to Clay Basket." His voice broke and he sobbed. "They beat me, and they made her watch. They shot me in the knees so I couldn't walk, then they made me crawl. But that wasn't enough for them. They put balls through my ankles and shoulder. And Belker finished the job by stabbing me."

"What about that dagger you had?" Shakespeare inquired.

"I always keep one hid under my shirt for emergencies," Nelson said. "I knew they'd kill me right off if I tried to draw it, so I waited, hoping Galt would come close enough for me to kill him. But he never did." His mouth twitched. "I remember how it felt when Belker's knife plunged into my back, then everything went black. The next I knew, you were turning me over." He stared at McNair. "You be careful of that Belker. He's a natural-born killer and he has a wicked streak a yard wide."

Nate had encountered the type before. "I'll take care of him personally," he said.

"Thanks," Nelson said, turning his head until his left cheek rested on the ground. Almost immediately his body went completely limp as he succumbed to the deep sleep of utter exhaustion.

"Like I told you, an honest man," Shakespeare commented rather sadly.

"Do either of those names he mentioned ring familiar to you?" Nate asked. "I seem to recall having heard of Belker somewhere before."

"You probably have," Shakespeare said. "Two years ago at the Rendezvous there was a wrestling match that got ugly. Both men grabbed their knives and went at it tooth and nail. Belker was one of them."

"The one who won," Nate said, remembering. "There was talk for a while of kicking him out of camp and not letting him attend again, but nothing ever came of it."

"Galt I've heard of also," Shakespeare disclosed. "He was trapping partner with a man named Wilson. About four years back they headed north into Blackfoot country and only Galt returned. He spread the word that the Blackfeet had lifted Wilson's hair."

"Everyone believed him?"

"No one had cause to do otherwise. Of course, now that I look back, I remember that Galt had a lot of furs to sell."

"Maybe that's where he got his start," Nate speculated. "For some reason or another he killed Wilson and took Wilson's peltries. When he learned how easy it was to get away with it, he must have figured he'd found the perfect way to get rich quick."

"He's about to learn differently."

Nate touched Nelson's hot brow. "He has a high fever. Do you really think he can pull through?"

"Can't say for sure. I have to dress those stab wounds next. If I can find the right herbs, I'll be able to make a poultice that should help some." Shakespeare gingerly examined the broken shoulder. "I do know he doesn't have any chance at all if we leave him."

"If we stay here too long, what will happen to Clay Basket?"

"You know the answer to that as well as I do," Shakespeare said. "Here." He shifted so he was straddling Nelson's upper arm. "Lend me a hand setting this bone."

Horrifying images of the fate facing Clay Basket bothered Nate as he worked. He kept thinking of his own wife, and how he would feel if the same thing had happened to Winona. Once the wounds were crudely bandaged and Pepin had a minty broth simmering on the fire, Nate stood and declared, "I'm going after them. The two of you catch up when you can."

"You're being hasty," Shakespeare said.

Pepin, who had been filled in after bringing the horses from the spring, nodded. "I agree with *Carcajou*. We are all in this together."

"I won't do anything stupid and get myself killed," Nate said. "I'll just keep an eye on them until you show up. And who knows? Maybe I'll have a chance to save the Crow woman."

"I'll go with you," Pepin offered.

"No," Nate said, dreading the Canadian's fiery temper would land them all in trouble. "If Nelson gets his strength back, it'll take both of you to bring him along. I'll do this alone."

"I don't like it," Shakespeare said.

"Neither do I, but we don't have much choice."

Pepin grumbled, and Shakespeare offered a few more objections, but in five minutes Nate was on the trail. He didn't admit as much to them, but his main reason for hurrying on ahead was specifically to rescue Clay Basket. Once the cutthroat gang stopped for the day, she'd be in for a terrifying ordeal. Nate was going to catch up to them before dark and spare her from a fate worse than death.

The tracks were plain to see. Apparently Galt and company were growing cockier the longer their bloody spree continued, because they hadn't even bothered to make any effort to throw off possible pursuit. Nate was grateful for their oversight since he could fairly fly in their wake.

Once again Nate resorted to the Comanche tactic of constantly changing horses, which he did once every hour no matter how tired a particular animal might be. In this way he kept his mounts fresh, able to cover ground swiftly. Small wonder, then, that by the middle of the afternoon he spotted a long line of riders in the distance. Instantly he angled into pines, and from then on until nearly sunset he shadowed the band, never narrowing the gap for fear of being spotted.

Galt's route was taking the killers steadily lower, and from the direction of travel Nate had a hunch they were making for the Green River region so as to be there early for the upcoming Rendezvous.

Twilight's gray veil shrouded the landscape when Nate saw an orange glow three-quarters of a mile off. Galt had finally made camp. Nate reined up, stepped from the stirrups, and hid the horses in heavy brush before venturing to a hill that overlooked the campfire.

The camp had been made in a shallow basin filled with grass watered by a crystal-clear pool. From a vantage point under a tree on a slope above, Nate enjoyed an unobstructed view of the activities taking place. One man was breaking and feeding small limbs to the fire. Another had the task of watering their many horses. Three men were sitting around doing nothing, while a fourth was hovering near a pretty Indian woman in a buckskin dress whose black hair flowed to her ankles: Clay Basket. She was making their supper.

Nate could not see their faces very well. Beyond noting that all the men were bearded and dressed much like trappers everywhere, he saw little of interest. Clay Basket, however, was a genuine beauty, not over 20 years of age to judge by her youthful appearance, with a noble bearing that spoke eloquently of her contempt for her abductors.

Deciding to sneak closer for a better look, Nate rose and picked his way down the slope. The wind was blowing to the southeast, so he wasn't worried about the horses picking up his scent. All he had to be concerned about was blundering into the open and being seen, or so he thought until he rounded a boulder the size of a carriage just as another man came around the boulder from the other side. Too late, Nate realized there had only been six men in camp, not seven. Too late, he saw this seventh cutthroat point a rifle at him and cock the hammer.

Chapter Nine

Nate King began to jerk his own rifle up, but realized instantly he would be shot if he tried anything, so he held himself still as the cutthroat walked toward him wearing a quizzical expression. His mind racing, Nate plastered a welcoming smile on his face and blurted out, "You're white! Then I'm safe at last! Am I glad to see you!" He knew his fate would be sealed if the band of bloodthirsty killers suspected he was after them; his life depended on convincing them he was totally harmless.

"Are you now?" the man responded suspiciously. Halting a few yards off, he scrutinized Nate from head to toe. "Who the hell are you and what are you doing spying on our camp?"

"Spying?" Nate laughed long and loud. "I just saw the smoke from a fire and was working my way close enough to see if I'd found whites or Indians. After what I've been through, I had to be sure before I showed myself."

"You haven't told me your name."

"Jess Smith," Nate lied. Hiding his identity seemed like a good idea. He was fairly well known among the trapping fraternity, and he had a widespread reputation for being an honest, forthright man in all his dealings. Should the killers learn the truth, they'd fear the worst and slay him on the spot. "What's yours?"

"Roarke," the man said. He scanned the forest. "Are you all alone?"

"That I am," Nate said. "My two partners were captured by the Blackfeet two days ago and I've been running from the devils ever since."

"Blackfeet? In this area?" Roarke didn't like the news.

"Yep. They can't be more than a day behind me if they're still on my trail," Nate said. He nodded at the other man's gun. "There's no need to cover me, friend. We're on the same side. It's us against them, isn't it?"

Roarke lowered his rifle, but only slightly, and motioned for Nate to precede him. "You go first, mister. My friends will want to hear this."

A crawling sensation broke out all over Nate's skin as he headed for the camp. All eyes were on him the moment he appeared, and the renegades gathered in a group to await him. None were men he knew, but he was able to pick the deadly Belker out of the bunch by the exceptionally long knife Belker wore. Stout, hairy, and grimy, Belker had the aspect of an undersized but ferocious black bear.

Nate noticed Clay Basket at the fire, watching him. He studiously paid no attention to her, since any interest he showed might arouse suspicion. Bestowing his phony smile on the group, he called out, "Howdy, gents! What a sight for sore eyes you are!" None of them answered him. A few whispered back and forth, and each one had a hand close to a weapon when Nate stopped and regarded them with what he hoped was a convincing imitation of heartfelt relief. "I never thought I'd set eyes on another trapping party again!"

Roarke halted behind Nate, and to one side. "This here is Jess Smith. He says he's on the run from Blackfeet."

"Oh?" said a skinny man sporting a wicked scar on his left cheek and three pistols jammed under his belt.

"That's right," Nate declared good-naturedly. "Like I told your friend here, a war party jumped Bill, Adam, and me two days ago. I saw old Bill go down with a lance in his shoulder, and Adam was set upon by three whooping warriors and taken alive. I've been on the run ever since."

"How is it that you escaped?" the skinny man asked.

"Sheer luck," Nate said. "I was answering Nature's call, and I'd just gone into the brush when I spotted one of the Blackfeet peeking at me from over a log. I gave a yell, but it was too late. They were already swarming into our camp, so I bolted." Nate shook his head as if in amazement at his own good fortune. "I tell you, the Good Lord must have been watching over me! Arrows and lances were raining down thicker than hail, yet I didn't get so much as a scratch."

"Remarkable," the skinny one said. "But I've heard of it happening before. Hell, once the Bloods came after me, shooting and firing until they ran out of bullets and arrows, and I still got away." Grinning, he offered his hand. "The name is Ira Galt. I'm the booshway of this here outfit."

"Pleased to meet you," Nate said, hiding his revulsion. "Any chance of another Mountanee Man getting himself a bite to eat and some coffee? I don't mind telling you I'm starved to death."

"It'll be a while before the grub is ready, but you're welcome to join us," Galt said. "Never let it be said we don't show hospitality to a brother trapper." Draping an arm over Nate's shoulder, he steered him toward the fire.

The others had relaxed. One of them chuckled. Another winked at a companion.

"Are you partial to kinnikinnick?" Galt asked Nate. "We've got plenty to share."

"Thank you, no. I never did pick up the tobacco habit."

"No? Most do sooner or later. How long have you been trapping?"

"A year, or thereabouts," Nate said.

Galt's dark eyes raked Nate from head to toe. "Really? I would have expected you to be an old hand."

Nate saw Clay Basket staring at him. Since they were making straight for her, he couldn't very well continue to act as if she didn't exist. Consistent with his acting the friendly fool, he commented, "My goodness! A woman! I haven't seen one of those in a coon's age."

"She's mine," Galt said, his harsh tone belying his grin. "So don't be getting any notions."

"I have a wife in the States," Nate said. "She'd shoot me if she caught me so much as looking at another woman."

"Just so you know how things are," Galt said. "Clay Basket is her name, and she's the best damn cook this side of the Divide."

"Do tell," Nate said, trying to sound suitably impressed even though he knew there hadn't been time for the Crow woman to prepare a single meal for the band since being abducted. "I can hardly wait to fill my belly."

Galt indicated a spot close to the flames. "Have a seat and we'll chaw a spell."

Easing down, Nate set eyes on dozens of bundles of prime peltries lying over near the horses. He let his eyes go wide and exclaimed, "Land sakes alive! You gents must be the best trappers around! You've enough hides there to set all of you up as kings!"

"Not quite," Galt said, laughing. "But there's no denying the past two seasons have been the best ever for us. We were raising so many beaver a day, at one point I thought my elbows would give out."

"So you're on your way to the Rendezvous?" Nate casually asked.

"That we are. We'll get there early and wait for the caravan to show."

"I envy you," Nate said. "I've lost everything but the clothes on my back. This trapping business isn't at all what it's cracked up to be. Between the weather, the Indians, and the animals, it's a wonder a body lives out his first year."

"Thinking of quitting?"

"Yes," Nate said. "I'm going back to New York and take up accounting like my pa wanted."

"Accounting is a nice, safe profession," Galt said, smirking. "The worst you'll have to worry about is smearing ink on a page."

Nate leaned the Hawken against a leg and held his hands out to the flames. Out of the corner of one eye he observed Clay Basket cutting up a doe. Out of the other eye he saw Roarke hovering in the background. The rest were taking seats around the fire. He was, in effect, hemmed in, as effectively as if they had built a fence around him.

"Ain't I seen you somewhere before?" Belker suddenly inquired. He was directly across from Nate, his right hand idly resting on the hilt of his big knife.

"It's possible," Nate said. "I was at the Rendezvous last year. Were you?"

"Yep," Belker said, "but I don't think it was then. Another time, maybe?"

"I've only been to one Rendezvous," Nate responded. "If you've seen me, that's where it was."

Belker's forehead creased and he tapped a finger on his knife. "I suppose."

It was like being the lone coyote among a pack of ravenous wolves. Nate was acutely aware of the cold, probing eyes fixed on him, but he didn't let on that he was in the least bit bothered. A plan was taking shape, a daring scheme that would result in the freeing of Clay Basket and reunite him with his friends, provided all went well. If not, he'd wind up like Nelson or Pointer, a most unappealing prospect.

In order to carry out his idea, Nate needed to convince the cutthroats he was no threat to them whatsoever. So he smiled and babbled about his limited trapping experience, about the problems he had faced and how few beaver he had caught.

The latter perked Galt's interest. "What about your friends? Did they have many furs?"

"About two hundred and ten, as I recall," Nate said, adding, "They were more experienced than I was." He glanced at the ring of faces, at the greed reflected by the firelight. "But now the Blackfeet have laid claim to them."

"What a waste," Galt said.

"True enough," Nate agreed. "Over a thousand dollars worth of hides gone, just like that." He snapped his fingers for emphasis.

"A thousand dollars," one of the men repeated longingly.

Galt thoughtfully scratched his scrawny beard. "How many Blackfeet did you say there were?"

"I didn't," Nate answered. He disliked the direction the talk was taking. The renegades were so eager to add to their spoils, they just might seriously consider going after the Blackfeet to get the extra pelts. In which case Nate had to discourage them. "There were over a dozen shrieking braves I saw with my own eyes and more off in the brush. Too many for one man to handle, which is why I lit out of there like my hind end was ablaze." He lowered his hands so he could readily grab his pistols if need be. "Too many for even an outfit this large to tackle."

"Sounds that way," Galt said, and cursed. "Too bad, Smith. We'd have liked to do the neighborly thing and help you reclaim your hides."

"That's awful decent of you," Nate said, continuing the charade. "But I wouldn't want complete strangers to lose their lives on my account. It's better this way anyway. I'm not cut out for the mountain life."

"Some are, some aren't," Galt said, and the issue was dropped.

Clay Basket stepped to the fire, a large pot and tripod in her hands. She pointedly looked at Nate, and because he had glanced up on hearing her footsteps, their eyes locked. For a fleeting second Nate thought he read an eloquent appeal for help in hers, yet all he could do was smile dumbly and act as if nothing was wrong. A flicker of disappointment etched her face as she bent to set up the tripod, and Nate deliberately gazed at the brightening stars.

Nate had to admire her courage. Here she was, in the clutches of the men who had attacked the man she loved, at their complete mercy, her life forfeit if she gave them any grief, yet she had the poise of a princess. Small wonder Nelson had been smitten by her.

"Hurry it up with the food, woman," Galt growled. "We're hungry, damn it."

Clay Basket wasn't intimidated. She finished arranging the tripod, hung the pot, and moved off.

"Squaws!" Galt chuckled and jabbed his elbow into Nate's ribs. "They can't hold a candle to white women. Lazy, uppity biddy hens is all they are."

"I wouldn't know," Nate said, though in truth he considered his Shoshone wife a competent, hardworking woman, and every inch a lady. Arching his back, he slowly stretched, turning his head to the right and left as he did, which gave him the opportunity to study the camp. The horses were to the south, strung in a long row. Saddles and parfleches were nearby, to the right of the mountain of peltries. To the east reared dense forest. The same to the north. To the west was the hill Nate had descended before being caught by Roarke. Which reminded him. What had Roarke been doing up there?

Nate half turned and discovered Roarke was gone. He nodded at Galt and asked, "Where did our friend get to?"

"To make a circuit of our camp. As you learned the hard way, it doesn't pay to let your guard down in this country. We always survey the countryside before we turn in."

"A smart practice," Nate said. "I wish we'd done the same."

Again Clay Basket returned, this time holding a wooden spoon with which she stirred the contents of the pot. Again Nate had to ignore her, although it pained him to do so. He figured she took him for the biggest fool in all Creation, as did her captors, and for the time being the illusion served his purpose admirably.

The renegades loosened up and talked about matters of no special consequence. Nate contributed little. When the stew was done, he ate heartily, two heaping helpings and part of a third. Nate often caught Galt lecherously ogling Clay Basket, and wondered if the cutthroat would try to force her to submit with him present.

And Nate had another concern. Would the renegades let him live or see fit to slay him when the whim struck? Countless corpses were testimony to their callous lust for money, yet he had nothing of great value. Nor did he have a pretty woman to catch the eye of Galt, as Tim Nelson had. No, he reflected, the killers might be inclined to let him be, if for no other reason than to show up anyone who might later point the finger of blame at any of them in connection with the murders. They might say something along the lines of: "See? Jess Smith spent time with us and we didn't kill him? So how dare you accuse us of going around killing every trapper we met?"

Regardless, Nate never let his vigilance down for a minute. When he was eating, one hand or the other was always next to a pistol. When drinking coffee, it was the same. He kept the different renegades in sight at all times, and when one or another went off into the brush, he never turned his back to that part of the forest.

Eventually Roarke showed up.

"Anything?" Galt asked.

"No campfires, no smoke, nothing. If the Blackfeet are after Smith, we'll be long gone before they show."

Galt and two of his men walked over to the peltries, and Galt selected a grassy spot on which the pair began constructing a conical structure of limbs and brush similar to the makeshift forts used by the Blackfeet on occasion. This one was smaller, suitable for two people at the most. Nate didn't need to ask who the structure was for, and he couldn't help but see Clay Basket's apprehension.

It ruined everything. Nate had hoped to wait until the cutthroats were asleep, then spirit the Crow woman to safety. Now he had to change his plan and embark on a riskier venture: to spirit her away right from under their noses before she was forced to go into the fort with Galt.

Doing his best not to be obvious about it, Nate kept watch over Clay Basket, always noting her position in relation to the forest and the horses in case a chance presented itself.

None did. The renegades bossed her around freely, keeping her busy doing minor chores such as fetching them coffee or jerky and gathering fuel for the fire. A killer always went with her when she went after branches, and hovered over her in camp like a hawk over its prey.

Nate was so preoccupied with watching Clay Basket that he didn't realize someone had addressed him until a hand clamped onto his shoulder and he twisted to see Galt eyeing him critically. "What?" he blurted out.

"I said," Galt repeated slowly, "what are we going to do about you?"

"How do you mean?"

"We don't have any extra horses to spare. All the pack animals are carrying as many peltries as they can, so we can't double up the loads." Galt stared at the animals. "You could ride double with one of us until we get to the Rendezvous site. Would that do you?"

"I'd be very grateful."

"We don't mind the company," Galt went on as if he hadn't heard, "but never forget that I'm the boss here and what I say goes. If I want you to lend a hand with the work, I expect you to chip in."

"That's only fair," Nate said, adopting his fake smile. "Hunting, cooking, chopping wood, you name it, I'll do what I can."

"There should be more folks like you," Galt said, the corners of his eyes crinkling. "Most don't know the first thing about gratitude nowadays."

Strange words, Nate reflected, coming from a confirmed murderer. He nodded and responded with: "How true. You've hit the old nail on the head. One of the reasons I left the States was because I'd grown so fed up with the cold way people in New York City treated others. I wanted something different."

"So did I," Galt said softly. "But the first few years I was out here, nothing went right for me. I was like you. Barely caught enough beaver to stake me for the next year. Had brushes with the Bloods and the Piegans. Nearly lost my hair more times than I care to remember."

"Yet you stuck with it." Nate bobbed a chin at the furs. "And now look! What's the secret of your success?"

"Hard work." Galt's smirk returned. "My pa always used to say that no matter what line of work a man picks, he should always do it the best he possibly can. I never thought much of his preaching when I was a kid, but now I see he had a point. I'm doing better than I ever dreamed I could by doing what I found I do best."

"Trapping," Nate said.

"What?" Galt glanced at him.

"Trapping beaver. Collecting pelts."

"Oh, yes. Collecting peltries is all I live for, you might say."

One of the men, Belker, had a coughing fit.

Nate played the innocent and leaned back, letting them think he didn't have any idea of the true meaning behind Galt's words. He glanced around, seeking Clay Basket, and was surprised to find she was gone. So was Roarke. They were probably off getting additional wood, he figured, and didn't think more of it until a sharp cry pierced the night and there was a loud crashing in the underbrush to the north.

Every last cutthroat leaped erect and had a gun ready when Clay Basket burst from the trees and halted to catch her breath. Her left cheek was bleeding from a small cut and there were red marks on her throat.

"What the hell!" Galt roared, racing over with his gang close on his heels.

Nate followed, but at a slower pace. He held back as Galt grabbed Clay Basket's wrist and gave her a vigorous shake.

"What happened to you, woman? Where's Roarke?"

"He tried to take me," Clay Basket said.

This was the first Nate had heard her speak, and he was struck by the musical lilt to her pleasant voice. Her English, while heavily accented, was almost as good as his wife's. Placing a finger on the hammer of his Hawken, he edged closer.

"Tried to take you?" Galt was saying. "In what way?"

"You know in what way."

"The son of a bitch!"

"I slapped him and he fell," Clay Basket said.

"I'll turn the bastard into a gelding!" Galt snarled. Drawing a knife, he plunged into the forest. His men stayed right with him.

In the excitement and anger of the moment, Nate and Clay Basket were left alone. He took a bound, snatched her hand, and declared, "There's no time to explain. I'm here to help you, to take you back to Nelson. You must come with me." Whirling, Nate headed northward, glancing once at the horses. He would much rather have cut them loose and stampeded them, but there were so many it would take a minute or two to drive every last animal off, and by then the renegades might return. He couldn't risk that. The only alternative, he felt, was to reach his own horses and ride like a bat out of hell back to where he had left his friends.

Clay Basket offered no protests. As fleet as a deer, she sprinted beside Nate, casting anxious eyes on the pines.

They crossed the open space, and were almost to the tree line when a strident shout erupted to their rear. Glancing around, Nate saw one of the killers.

"Galt! Galt! He's stealin' your woman, damn it! They're headin' west!"

Furious yells broke out. Nate raised his rifle to swat a limb aside as he sped into the woods. He could have shot the man who gave the warning, but he preferred to save the ball for when he would need it the most. Darting around a tree trunk, he ran flat out, Clay Basket matching his pace if not his stride. He was angling up the hill when the night thundered to the blast of a rifle and a searing pain lanced his left thigh.

Chapter Ten

Nate was knocked forward by the impact. He automatically let go of Clay Basket's hand as his left leg twisted and he fell, smacking onto his knee. Grimacing, he looked down at his thigh. In the dark, the spreading stain on his leggings seemed almost black. He gingerly touched the wound, tracing a furrow several inches long and less than a quarter of an inch deep. Nasty, but not life-threatening.

"Can you stand, Jess?" Clay Basket asked, sliding her hands under his arms. "I will help you."

"I can manage," Nate assured her. He pushed upright, took her hand again, and resumed running.

"You're bleeding!"

"I'd rather be bleeding than dead."

And dead Nate would be if Galt had his way. Nate could hear the enraged renegade bellowing orders, instructing the cutthroats to fan out, to spare the woman no matter what. As for his fate, that was sealed if the killers got him in their clutches. They'd either slay him outright, or more likely, drag him to their camp so they could give him the same treatment they had given their lengthy list of victims.

Nate tried to remember exactly how far they had to go to reach the black stallion and his other mounts. For the life of him, he couldn't. Was it 300 yards? Or 400? He knew exactly where the animals were tethered, but he had been concentrating on the camp as he went down the hill and hadn't kept track of the distance.

The renegade trappers were coming on fast, as evidenced by the crackling of brush and the pad of rushing feet. Nate shot a glance over his shoulder, and counted four figures strung out in a ragged line from north to south. They were at the bottom of the hill, starting up.

Surely, Nate reflected, Galt would have every last man taking part in the chase. Where, then, were the missing three? Had Galt stayed behind? Was Roarke dead?

Nate spied a log in his path. "Jump!" he whispered, and did just that. Clay Basket matched his feat, and side by side they alighted and dashed onward. To Nate's dismay, he then heard what he feared the most, the drumming of heavy hoofs. A look showed a pair of horsemen galloping in determined pursuit. Already the riders had passed the four men on foot.

Being caught was inevitable. There wasn't a man alive who could outrun a horse, especially on a hill. Nate saw a thicket to his left. Slowing, he pulled Clay Basket down next to him as he stooped to enter the prickly maze. The hoofbeats were drawing rapidly closer and closer. Nate squeezed through a gap and squatted in a small enclosed space. Clay Basket joined him. Between them there wasn't enough room left for either to lift an arm.

Seconds later the monstrous shapes of the riders, looming in the night like ancient creatures called centaurs Nate had once read about, appeared. They reined up ten feet from the thicket and one of them vented his spleen.

"Damn it all! Where the hell are they? I thought I saw them at this very spot a few seconds ago!"

Nate was surprised to recognize Roarke's voice.

"Keep it down!" the second man hissed. "Do you want them to hear you?"

"What difference does it make? They know we're here," Roarke replied testily. "And we're going to find them, even if we have to stay up all night."

"You're just mad because that squaw walloped you good and made you look like an idiot."

"You'd be mad too, Sterret, if she'd caught you off guard like she did me. Stinking treacherous females!"

"Were I you, I'd be more worried about whether Galt believes your story. If he asks her, and she sticks by her tale of you trying to get up her dress, Galt will skin you alive."

"I'm not scared of him," Roarke said with less than sterling confidence. "Now come on! We have to find the bitch!"

Nate watched the pair gallop westward. When they were gone, he leaned over and smiled. "Too bad you didn't bust his skull wide open."

"He lies," Clay Basket said. "He attacked me first and I slapped him, just as I said. He fell and pulled his knife, so I ran back. I would rather have gone deeper into the woods, but I was afraid he would shoot me if I tried."

"You've done right fine so far," Nate complimented her. "Nelson would be proud of you."

"He is alive, then?" Clay Basket asked anxiously. "You were speaking with a straight tongue?"

"I left him with friends who are trying to patch him up."

Clay Basket's eyes shimmered in the dim light. "You do not know how happy you have made me. I believed he was dead."

"We have to get you—" Nate began, and froze on discerning more voices. Some of the renegades on foot were approaching. He tensed, lowering a hand to a pistol since the flintlocks would be easier to use in the confined space and at short range were just as accurate as the Hawken.

"—ain't seen hide nor hair of them. I say we go get horses and torches."

"And I say we keep lookin' until Galt tells us otherwise. He's riled up, and you know how he gets when he's riled. Anyone who complains is liable to wish they hadn't."

Nate could see one of the cutthroats moving at the edge of the thicket. Would they think to check inside it? he wondered. Fingers touched his arm and squeezed. Clay Basket was terrified, as her low gasp proved when the cutthroat stopped. The man faced the thicket and bent down.

"What is it?" another asked.

"Thought I heard something," the man said, swinging from side to side.

"Probably a damn rabbit," said the other. "They wouldn't go in there with us on their trail."

The cutthroat examining the thicket grunted. "I guess not." He slowly straightened, motioned at his companion, and both were soon lost in the murky vegetation.

"Stay close to me," Nate cautioned, easing onto his elbows so he could crawl to the opening and peek out. A cool breeze stirred the trees and the grass. He scanned the shadows, saw no one, then eased out and helped Clay Basket to stand.

"Which way?" she wanted to know.

That was the crucial question. To go west would be flirting with death, yet to the west was where the horses waited. Going east would take them to the basin and Galt. Nate stared southward and northward, debating, and he had not quite made up his mind when the metallic rasp of a gun hammer being cocked sent a tingle down his spine.

"Don't move, either of you!"

Two of the renegades strode from cover, the same pair who had stopped next to the thicket. The taller of the duo snickered and remarked, "I knew I saw something in there!"

"That you did, Johnny," said the other.

Nate had his right arm at his side, holding the Hawken. His left arm was slightly behind him, out of sight of the approaching killers. Relying on the dark to blanket his movements, he inched his finger to his butcher knife and clasped the hilt.

"Drop that long gun, you ornery greenhorn," the one named Johnny commanded. "Then step back and put your arms in the air where we can see them."

"And don't try nothin' clever unless you want to eat lead," his companion said. "I've got a ball in this here barrel with your name on it."

Nate had no choice but to obey, but he didn't do exactly as they wanted. He slowly lowered the Hawken's stock to the ground, exaggerating his motion. Both renegades kept their eyes on the rifle in case he should suddenly reverse his grip and try to bring it to bear. With their attention on the gun, neither noticed the sleight of hand Nate resorted to, for while they were momentarily distracted by the movement of his right arm, he slowly raised his left arm, drawing his knife as he did and holding it flush against his forearm so they couldn't see it. He then elevated his right arm and stood awaiting further directions. "Satisfied?"

"Sure am," Johnny said, coming closer. "I thought for certain you'd do something stupid and get yourself killed."

"Which would spoil the surprises Galt has in store for you," said his companion.

Johnny wagged his rifle. "George, take his pistols before he gets any contrary notions. And his tomahawk and knife too."

Nodding, George warily stepped forward and stopped to the right of Nate. He touched the barrel of his rifle to Nate's stomach and said, "You heard the man. Hand 'em over. And remember, no tricks."

"Don't worry," Nate said meekly to make them think he would do as they wanted. "I'm not looking to get myself killed."

"Then you shouldn't of run off with the squaw," George said, and laughed.

Nate glanced down at George's rifle as he slowly reached for his right flintlock. The rifle wasn't cocked. He glanced at Johnny and saw that Johnny's rifle was leveled at his midsection but not at any specific spot. As risky as it was, there might not be a better time. So, when his finger curled around his pistol, he tensed his body and ever so slowly began to ease the pistol clear.

George looked at Johnny and snorted. "Well-behaved greenhorn, ain't he?"

And in that instant when Johnny was focused on George, Nate sprang into action, whipping the pistol from under his belt and cocking the hammer in a single smooth draw while simultaneously he firmed his hold on the butcher knife and arced his left arm across his chest, spearing it around and in. Both killers were swift to react: Johnny to raise his rifle a bit higher, George to begin to turn back toward Nate.

Nate fired before Johnny did, the heavy-caliber flintlock belching smoke and bucking in his hand. At almost the same moment he twisted and sliced his big blade into George's chest, just below the sternum. George clutched at the knife, then tried to cock his rifle. Nate, pivoting, slammed his pistol into the renegade's temple, and George dropped the rifle and staggered, his knees buckling. The butcher knife jerked loose, dripping crimson drops. A second blow brought George down. Nate, fearing the other cutthroat might not be mortally wounded, spun, but he need not have worried.

The man called Johnny was flat on his back, his lifeless eyes fixed on the heavens, a hole in his chest bubbling blood.

Nate turned back to George to finish him off. Shouts in the forest to the west changed his mind, since it meant the rest were on their way and might get there before he could escape with the woman. He slid the butcher knife into its sheath without bothering to wipe the blade, wedged the pistol under his belt, and stooped to grab the Hawken. "They'll be on us quick. We have to hurry," he said, offering his hand to the Crow.

Clay Basket paused, looked down at George's rifle, and hastily retrieved it. "I will keep up," she pledged.

A horse and rider were barreling through the undergrowth less than 30 yards away. Nate whirled and fled once again, southward this time, skirting the thicket and crossing a moonlit glade. Clay Basket might have been part of him, so smoothly did she run at his side. When he swerved, she did. When he vaulted over a log, she did the same without breaking stride or causing him to either. Whatever he did, she duplicated it flawlessly. They ran in virtual silence thanks to the thick carpet of pine needles underfoot.

"Quince! Roarke! The rest of you! Over here!"

Nate knew that Johnny and George had been found. Soon the others would be in pursuit, provided they could track at night. Some Indians could. The average trapper became a fair hand at it out of necessity, but few became adept enough to rival the Indians. Then Nate thought of Belker, and something told him that there was a man who could track an ant over solid rock.

At least, Nate reflected, he had reduced the odds by one, possibly two, since if George lived he would be in no shape to pose a threat. Which left Galt, Belker, Roarke, Sterret, and Quince. Nate needed to remember those names. If he survived, if the renegades got away, he would let all the other trappers at the upcoming Rendezvous know who had been part of the bloodthirsty band. The word would spread like wildfire to all friendly Indian tribes, and be taken back to St. Louis with the caravan traders. Galt and company would find themselves the objects of the biggest manhunt in the history of the frontier. Their lives wouldn't be worth a pile of buffalo chips.

Galt was smart. He had to realize that. So Nate couldn't count on the renegades giving up easily. They'd scour the countryside for miles around, take days if need be. Evading them was going to be a chore.

Just how much of a chore became apparent when Nate heard the pounding of hoofs. Darting behind a pine, he crouched down in the nick of time. A pair of renegades galloped past, not 50 feet to the east. They neither slowed nor spoke and were presently out of sight.

"That was close," Nate whispered in Clay Basket's ear. "We'd best sit tight for a minute. They just might swing on around."

"You are very brave, Jess Smith. I can never thank you for what you have done."

"King. Nate King," Nate corrected her. "I gave them a different name because they might have heard of me."

"I do not understand."

"If they'd known who I really was, they'd have killed me as soon as I stepped into their camp."

"Are you a friend of the Blanket Chief?"

That was the Indian name for Jim Bridger, without a doubt the most widely respected trapper alive. His word carried more weight with the Indians than the word of practically all other white men combined. Only Shakespeare

McNair had an equal reputation. "I am," Nate admitted. "And I'm an even closer friend of the man your people know as Wolverine Killer."

Clay Basket was trying to study his features in the darkness. "How else are you known?" she inquired.

"The Shoshones and Flatheads call me Grizzly Killer."

"I have heard of you. Once, many moons ago, Wolverine Killer and you visited the village of our high chief, Long Hair. It was said you brought him horses and eagle feathers to restore the honor of a warrior who died in disgrace."

Nate had nearly forgotten about that day. "He was a good man. I owed it to him," he answered, and let it go at that.

To the southeast the two riders could be heard sweeping the area. Nate elected to stay put for the time being since they were safe from detection.

"Is it true you are an adopted Shoshone?" Clay Basket whispered.

"It is."

"My Nelson wants my people to adopt him," she said proudly. "I hope they will agree."

"He loves you very much," Nate mentioned. "When we found him, he told us to forget about him and go after you. Your safety came first. He didn't care about himself."

Clay Basket's head bowed, her hair falling across her face. "My heart is his forever. I could not live without him."

Just then Nate stared northward and caught a hint of someone moving. He put a hand to her mouth and pulled her lower. The stout figure glided nearer, a lone renegade bent at the waist, examining the ground. Nate didn't need to see the man clearly to know who it was: Belker, he of the huge knife and sinister eyes.

Nate put a hand on his left pistol. He'd let Belker get closer, right up to the pine in fact, and fire at almost point-blank range so he couldn't miss. Then there would be two down and only five to deal with. But the cutthroat thwarted him.

Belker halted 20 feet away and bent down to touch the ground. His head snapped up, but he looked to the southeast, not at the pine. For several seconds he was like a statue. Unexpectedly, he turned and headed due west, dashing into the trees.

The move perplexed Nate. Why, if Belker had been tracking them, had the killer gone in an entirely different direction? And why had Belker stared to the southeast? Nate did the same, and saw the two riders returning. Spaced a dozen yards apart, they were searching around every bush, under every tree.

"Damn," Nate whispered. He gestured at Clay Basket, turned, and bore to the southwest. There was plenty of cover, so he had no difficulty in eluding the horsemen. Once he felt they had covered enough ground, he rose and resumed running.

Nate often thought of being abroad in the forest at night as a dream-like experience. The delicate play of shadows and pale moonlight lent the terrain an eerie aspect heightened by the often total silence and complete lack of wildlife. It was so different from the same forest during the day when the sun blazed and the wild creatures were singing or scampering about, when the forest was so vibrant with life.

Ten minutes elapsed. Nate stopped at the edge of a meadow to reload the spent pistol and to allow Clay Basket to catch her breath. Somewhere close at hand an owl hooted.

"They will keep looking for a long time, will they not?" she asked.

"Yes."

"Do you have horses?"

Nate nodded as he opened the flap on his ammo pouch. "But the only way to get to them without attracting attention is to swing wide to the west. If we push ourselves, and if we don't run into any problems, we can reach the spot by dawn."

"Then let us keep going. I want to see my Nelson."

"Whatever you want."

Nate had a course worked out in his head. Since the renegades were concentrating on a narrow area, all he had to do was outflank them. He did so by bearing to the southwest for an hour and then turning westward. Besides a few crickets and coyotes, they had the night to themselves.

"Do you have a woman, Grizzly Killer?" Clay Basket asked at one point.

"Yep. The prettiest Shoshone ever born," Nate boasted, grinning. "And we have two sprouts too. A boy and a girl."

"Do you ever regret taking her for your wife?"

The unanticipated question prompted Nate to glance at her. "Never. Why would you ask such a thing?"

"I sometimes think Nelson will one day believe he made a mistake and he will go back to his own people."

"If you'd heard him urging us to save you, you'd know how silly you sound," Nate told her. "I've never met a man anywhere more in love than he is. He'll stick by you through thick and thin."

"I hope so," Clay Basket declared.

The conversation made Nate think of his own wife, and he longed to be holding her in his arms again and inhaling the fragrant scent of her hair. As much as he enjoyed the life of a free trapper, there were certain drawbacks every trapper had to accept, one of them being long periods away from loved ones. He was about to remark as much to the Crow woman when there arose a loud crackling in the trees directly ahead.

Nate halted and motioned for her to do the same. He trained his Hawken on a dark blotch of trees, then crouched. Clay Basket imitated him, ready to back him up with the rifle she had taken from George.

The trees moved, some of the limbs swaying violently.

Nate saw, and blinked. Those limbs were seven or eight feet off the ground. Whatever was in there had to be enormous. Mentally, he ticked off a short list of likely creatures: an elk, a grizzly, or something smaller in the tree itself. Whatever it was suddenly grunted, a deep, guttural grunt such as a bear would make, only much deeper than any bear Nate had ever heard.

"What is it?" Clay Basket asked softly.

"I don't know," Nate admitted. Unbidden, he remembered the tale Pepin had told of the mysterious Canadian mammoth. He peered intently into the inky gloom, and swore he saw the vague outline of a gigantic beast standing on two legs. Yet when he closed his eyes a second and opened them again, the outline was gone.

"I thought I saw something," Clay Basket said.

Nate listened to the crackling as the strange animal moved about. The thing didn't seem to be in any great hurry to move on, so to avoid a confrontation, Nate took Clay Basket's wrist and slanted to the right to go around.

There was a crack, as of a tree limb being broken, followed by a disturbing silence.

Nate didn't stop. He wanted no part of the unknown creature. As he hurried along, he experienced the sensation of unseen eyes watching him, and the short hairs at the nape of his neck prickled. A glance at Clay Basket confirmed she was equally anxious. Frayed nerves, he figured. The two of them had been under a constant strain for so long that their minds were playing tricks on them.

After several minutes Nate allowed himself to relax. The

animal hadn't given chase, so they were safe. He surveyed the landscape, trying to guess their position in relation to where the horses were tied, and calculated they were a mile or more to the southwest. On all sides reared heavy timber, with a lot of downed trees and thick brush that would slow them down. They would be lucky if they reached the horses by first light, as he wanted to do.

Half an hour went by. Nate had the Hawken resting on his shoulder and was strolling along the bottom of a gulch they had stumbled on. Here there were fewer obstacles and the going was easier. He checked on Clay Basket, and saw her fiddling with a moccasin. And then, as he was partially turned toward her, there was the rattle of dirt on the gully slope, a swishing noise, and something heavy pounced on his back.

Chapter Eleven

Nate King's first thought, on hearing the rattle of the dirt, was that the creature they had encountered earlier had stalked them and was attacking him. He tried to spin, but was way too slow. The impact smashed him to the ground so hard the breath whooshed from his lungs. He felt the Hawken being torn from his grasp, and through a haze of pain he saw Clay Basket bringing her rifle to bear even as a sharp object gouged him in the side of the neck and a gruff voice spoke.

"Try it, squaw, and this son of a bitch dies!"

It was Belker! Nate realized, and tried to move, but the renegade was on his back, kneeling on him, pinning him in place. Clay Basket glanced at him, then at the killer. Reluctantly, she lowered her rifle and took a step back.

"How touching!" Belker quipped. "I knew there was more to this bastard than he let on. What, is he your lover?"

"He is a friend," Clay Basket answered indignantly.

"And I'm the king of England," Belker said. "The two of you didn't fool me for a minute. I saw the way he was watchin' you when he thought no one else would notice. Idiots!"

Nate was trying to get his right arm out from under him so he could reach for his tomahawk. He had almost succeeded when the knife point gouged deeper into his neck and a hand seized hold of his hair and yanked on his head.

"Try that, fool, and I'll slit you from ear to ear!" Belker hissed. He slid off Nate and stood, hauling Nate erect by the hair. "Give me any excuse and you're a dead man, no matter what Galt wants."

Nate was given a rough shove that sent him stumbling toward Clay Basket. He kept his balance, drew up short, and was poised to draw a pistol when he saw the renegade had already done so.

"Drop all your weapons, Smith. Nice and slow."

Only a fool resisted while staring down the barrel of a .55-caliber flintlock. Simmering with anger at being caught so handily, Nate removed all four of his belt weapons. The smirk on Belker's grimy face only aggravated him more.

"That's a good boy," the cutthroat taunted. "I knew you'd be reasonable about it." Chuckling, he wagged his pistol. "Now back up."

Nate's blood boiled as he helplessly watched Belker taking possession of their arms, and he wanted to kick himself for being so careless. He had to rein in a suicidal urge to make a mad dash at the renegade. Presently he was looking down the barrel of his own Hawken instead of a pistol.

"Next we march out and around to the top of this gully so I can fetch my rifle," Belker said. "Keep your hands where I can see them, because I assure you I have no qualms about shootin' either of you in the back if you give me the slightest cause."

Nate believed him. Turning, he allowed Clay Basket to go first. That way, he could block Belker's view of her if he had to. He tried to catch her eye and signal her with a bob of his head to let her know she should make a bid to escape if the opportunity presented itself, but she was staring at the ground, dejected. They retraced their steps to the mouth of the gully, and began climbing a gradual incline to the top.

"I've got to hand it to you, Smith," Belker commented. "You gave the others a merry chase. But then, they're not the tracker I am. I found your trail right away and almost blundered onto you when you were hiding behind that pine. Remember?"

Nate wasn't going to respond, but a sharp poke between the shoulder blades changed his mind. "I remember," he said sullenly.

"I knew the two of you were hidin' there, so I went off into the brush and waited for you to show yourselves. Then I followed you until I saw my chance. Pretty clever, huh?"

"Was that you in the trees?" Nate asked.

"What trees?"

"In that stand a while back, breaking limbs and making those sounds?"

"I don't know what you're talkin' about. I never got too close because I didn't want you spottin' me before I was ready to make my move."

Nate came to the rim of the gully. Grass and bushes grew to the very edge, and he was obliged to step around some of the latter as he followed Clay Basket toward the spot where Belker had jumped them from the rim. A germ of an idea formed, and he scanned the slope in front of them. He glanced back, measuring the distance between the renegade and him, and suppressed a grin.

"Have you ever seen someone have their belly slit and their innards ripped out?" Belker was saying. "I have. It ain't a sight for the squeamish." He snickered. "I expect I'll get to see it again when Galt starts in on you. Trust me, pilgrim. He's not the kind of man you want to rile. Something inside of him snaps and he goes all crazy. Why, once I saw him carve a man up so bad the man didn't hardly look human no more when Galt was done."

"I bet you've done your share," Nate remarked.

"Meaning?"

"I've heard about you, Belker. You're no saint."

The renegade chortled. "No, I ain't. I've planted a few jackasses in my time. But I always do the job neat and clean, not like Galt. He likes to see people suffer, likes to see them squirm and hear them beg for their lives. One time he reached inside a guy he'd cut open and pulled the fella's heart out with his bare hand. Lordy, was that a sight!"

Nate had slowed a bit so Clay Basket could gain a couple of yards on them. He didn't want her to be too close when he made his move.

"I swear that Galt was born wrong," Belker had gone on. "He should have been born a Blackfoot or an Apache instead of a white man. He'd have been right at home with them."

"And you don't mind riding with someone like him?"

"Mind, hell! He's making us rich, ain't he? I don't care how crazy he gets just so we keep on filling our pokes with fur money."

Another bush appeared in front of Nate, the largest yet, over three feet high. This time, instead of going around the plant on the left side, where the ground was level, he went around on the right side, where the slope dropped away to the bottom of the gully. Almost immediately the loose earth gave way under his foot and he started to slip.

"Not that way, damn you!" Belker bellowed.

Nate deliberately fell onto his stomach and clawed at the slope, pretending he was caught in gravity's grip, while at the same time he dug in his toes to arrest his descent. He also pretended to pay no attention at all to the renegade, who stepped close to the edge and glared down at him.

"Get back up here!"

"I'm trying," Nate lied, scrambling faster, his left hand moving closer and closer to Belker's legs each time he dug his fingers into the earth.

"Try harder, idiot." Belker motioned impatiently, and when he did the barrel of the Hawken swung to one side.

This was the moment Nate had been waiting for. Braced on his toes, he lunged upward, still pretending to be clawing at the slope when in reality he was diving at Belker's legs. His left arm looped around both of the cutthroat's ankles and with a tremendous heave he upended Belker and pulled.

Venting a string of oaths, the renegade plummeted over the edge, tumbling downward, one rifle flying but not the Hawken. Together they rolled to the very bottom, where Nate released his hold and seized the Hawken by the barrel. With a terrific wrench he gained control of the gun, but as he did it went off almost in his face.

"Damn you!" Belker roared, rising. His hand swooped to his belt and flashed out holding the long knife he favored. "To hell with Galt! I'm putting you under right here and now!"

Nate barely backed away quickly enough to avoid a wicked slash that would have gutted him. He swung the Hawken at Belker's head, but the wily killer ducked under the swing and stabbed at Nate's legs. Nate had to leap backward. As he did, Belker grasped the rifle barrel.

There they stood, not more than a yard apart, each with a hand on the Hawken, Belker waving his long knife in small circles in the air. "Think you're clever, don't you, smart boy?" he said mockingly. "Well, we'll see how clever you think you are after I cut out your tongue."

Nate didn't waste breath replying. He gave a tug on the Hawken, pulling Belker toward him, and leaped straight at the shorter man. His hand closed on the renegade's right wrist to keep the knife at bay while his knee drove into Belker's groin. They both toppled, Belker clamping his other hand on Nate's throat.

Back and forth they rolled, each struggling mightily to gain an advantage. Nate was amazed at the renegade's strength. Strive as he might, the knife edged ever nearer to his face.

Belker growled as he fought, much like the black bear he so resembled, his lips curled to reveal his clenched teeth. "You're mine! Hear me? Mine!" he cried.

Nate strained his utmost and pushed the renegade's arm back a few inches. Their rolling brought them up against the slope, with Nate on the bottom. Belker angled the razor-edged blade inward, seeking Nate's neck. Nate, in desperation, snapped his head forward, butting his brow into the cutthroat's nose. Something cracked, and Belker shrieked and tried to rise.

Coiling his legs, Nate rammed both feet into the renegade's midriff. Belker went flying rearward to crash onto his back in the middle of the gully. Nate pushed into a crouch and charged just as Belker was rising. His shoulder caught the killer in the side, bowling Belker over, but as Belker went down he cut upward with the knife, ripping Nate's buckskin shirt and slicing the skin.

They parted. Nate could feel blood trickling from his wound. He balled his fists and waited for his foe to make the next move.

Belker was in no hurry. Ready to strike, he held the knife at his waist. He was getting his breath back while letting the pain in his ribs subside. And too, he was studying Jess Smith more closely. For a greenhorn, Smith was a hellion. Or was Smith a greenhorn? Belker stared, and suddenly remembered the Rendezvous several years ago. "Damn! I knew I'd laid eyes on you before. You're Nate King, aren't you?"

Long ago Nate had learned not to talk when in a fight. Talking served as a distraction and might cost a man his life. So he simply nodded and circled to the right.

"I thought so!" Belker said. "That explains a lot! Wait until Galt hears."

Nate continued to slowly circle, planting each foot carefully.

"The great Grizzly Killer!" Belker said, and snorted. "Who would have thought it?" His brow puckered. "Wait a minute. You're married to some Shoshone bitch. What's this Crow squaw mean to you?"

Seldom had Nate fought anyone who talked so much. He saw a rock between them, and on an impulse he flicked out his foot, kicking the rock at the renegade, who stepped to the side. Nate kicked again, only this time a spray of dirt that made Belker raise an arm to protect his eyes. Instantly Nate leaped and gripped Belker's right wrist in both hands. Pivoting, Nate whirled, throwing every last ounce into a swing that propelled the cutthroat into the gully wall.

Belker landed on his back and endeavored to rise. Nate, taking swift strides, got there first and lashed out with his left foot. The long knife went sailing into the dark. Belker, incensed, reached for the tomahawk he had taken from Nate, but Nate closed and down they went again, punching one another furiously.

Nate landed a right to the jaw and received a left in the stomach. He blocked a flurry, then drove his left fist into Belker's cheek, splitting the flesh. Belker's forearm clubbed Nate on the ear. Nate connected, his knuckles flattening the renegade's lips. In unison they rose to their knees, slugging away all the while.

The blows were brutal, bone-wrenching. Nate shut out the agony and tried to knock the cutthroat out with a solid right to the jaw. It was like striking metal. Belker merely flinched. Nate took a punch to the temple that made him see stars. He pushed backward, shaking his head to recover, and was tackled about the chest. Once more he wound up flat on his back.

Belker seemed determined to end the fight at all costs. His fists were blurs as he pounded without letup.

Nate was losing and knew it. He brought his left arm high so his face would be spared, and shoved against the cutthroat with his right hand. Belker was immovable. Bucking his hips, Nate simultaneously twisted and threw the renegade off. His head swimming, he straightened, then froze upon hearing a click.

One of Nate's pistols was now aimed at his head. Belker grinned, wiped blood from the corner of his mouth, and said, "Enough of this. I should have shot you the minute I first saw you. Meet your Maker, King."

A single shot sounded, resembling a blast of thunder, echoing along the gully in both directions.

Belker's grin faded. He tried to lift an arm to touch the ragged cavity in his forehead, but couldn't. The pistol drooped, his arm sagged. His whole body went limp and he pitched forward.

Nate darted out of the way and stared down at the killer in bewilderment. A sigh drew his gaze to the rim, where Clay Basket was lowering the smoking rifle she had just used. Belker's own gun had been turned against him. "Thanks," Nate said softly. Absently, he brushed at the gore that had spattered the front of his shirt.

Clay Basket came down the slope, sliding half the way, the rifle employed as a crutch to keep her erect. In a swirl of dust she stopped and gazed at the man she had slain. "If ever a man deserved to die, he was one."

"You'll get no complaints from me," Nate assured her. He held up his hands and saw the skin peeled from his knuckles. Bruises and welts covered him from his face to his groin.

"Now we are safe, Grizzly Killer," Clay Basket said. "Now we can hurry to my Nelson."

"If none of his friends heard the shot," Nate observed. He would have liked to sit down and rest, but he had already grown careless once and wasn't about to make the same mistake again. Swiftly he scaled the east side of the gully and stood listening. No shouts sounded anywhere. The night was as quiet as a tomb.

"We were lucky," Nate said as he rejoined her. "We're too far away for them to have heard." Taking Belker's rifle from her, he loaded it and gave it back. He also gave her Belker's pistol and knife. His own weapons soon adorned his waist. Carrying the Hawken in one hand and George's rifle in the other, he resumed their interrupted trek at a faster clip.

Neither of them spoke for the longest while. The cut Nate had sustained stung terribly but wasn't life-threatening, so he ignored it. Which was typical, not just for him but for most trappers. Whiners and weaklings had no business being in the mountains. Those who fainted at the sight of blood were better off in the States where civilized society spared them from the grimmer realities of life.

Gradually the sky to the east lightened. Not much, but enough to signal the advent of dawn within the hour. Nate was extremely tired, and imagined Clay Basket felt the same. He had to admire her fortitude in holding up as well as she had, and he rated Tim Nelson a very fortunate man in having earned the love of such a remarkable woman. Back in the States there were many who looked down on Indians, who regarded Indians as somehow inferior to whites, as little better than animals. He'd often wondered if those people would change their minds if they could live with Indians for a while and get to know the so-called "savages" as they really were. Doing so had certainly changed his outlook. Ignorance, it seemed to him, was a prime breeding ground for hatred and bloodshed, and he thought it a shame that so many were afflicted with a lack of human understanding.

Out of consideration for Clay Basket, Nate halted on a rise and remarked, "Let's rest a few minutes. It won't do us any good to wear ourselves to a frazzle."

"If you want," she replied, not sounding very pleased by the delay.

Nate looked at her and debated whether to say something, whether to prepare her for the grim possibility that the man she loved might be dead. Tim Nelson, after all, had been in grave condition when Nate rode off. But when he saw her gazing westward, an eager gleam animating her eyes, he couldn't bring himself to shatter her hopes. Instead, he commented, "By tonight you should be back with Tim."

Clay Basket's throat bobbed. "He is all I think about." She grinned self-consciously. "I always thought I would one day marry a man from my own tribe. I never thought I would love a trapper."

"Love is strange that way," Nate agreed. "There's no telling when it will strike. If someone had told me when I was younger that I'd wind up taking a Shoshone woman as my wife, I'd have laughed right in their face."

"When this is over, maybe you and your wife would see fit to visit us."

"I'm sure she'd like that."

"I wish—" Clay Basket said, and abruptly stopped.

Nate turned and gazed in the same direction. An enormous mountain lion was descending the nearest mountain. The great cat was just below the snow line, barely visible crossing an open space. It moved with a fluid grace that was apparent even at that distance, and with the first pale glow of dawn dappling its tawny coat, the predator presented a stirring sight. "Lord, I love these mountains," Nate said to himself.

"So do I," Clay Basket said.

They watched until the mountain lion disappeared in high timber. Then Nate hefted the two rifles he held and resumed their hike. How different life had been back in New York City, he reflected, when the only wild creatures he had seen were stray dogs and cats and flocks of pigeons. Perhaps his city upbringing explained why he never tired of the wildlife in the wilderness. To see a grizzly or a buffalo or an eagle was always a thrill; each experience added a certain spice to his life that far surpassed anything he had ever known in civilization.

Presently Nate had a more pressing matter to consider. He had guided them by instinct, relying on his sense of direction to bring them right to where he had left his horses. He had roughly calculated the time it would take them, and had believed they would get there before the sun rose, but now, with the eastern sky growing steadily brighter, there was no sign of the hill he sought. Granted, he was approaching the spot from a different direction, but he had learned enough about noting and memorizing landmarks to be certain he would know the area when he saw it.

Halting, Nate studied the lay of the land. There was a mountain to the west, a hill to the north, and another to the northeast. One of those hills must be the one overlooking the basin in which the renegades had camped, but which one? Neither was familiar.

"Is something wrong?" Clay Basket inquired.

"Just getting my bearings," Nate said, striding to the northeast. Logic told him that must be the right hill, but when they came on a narrow creek he hadn't seen before, he began to doubt his judgment. Since the two of them hadn't had a drop to drink in many hours, they stopped and quenched their thirst. The water was cold, refreshing. Nate wiped a sleeve across his mouth when he was done. Then he splashed water on the wound in his thigh, which was smarting terribly and had swollen up, and on the cut he had sustained fighting Belker.

"That leg should be bandaged," Clay Basket remarked.

"When we have the time."

Across the creek Nate found fresh elk tracks, which was reassuring. If any of the cutthroats were in the area, the elk wouldn't have strayed from cover to drink. Still, he stayed alert as he wound through the forest toward the hill.

"How long will it take us to reach my Nelson?" Clay Basket asked.

"About four hours at the most."

"Is that all?" Clay Basket said, and smiled.

Nate studied the west slope of the hill. There was a certain pine he looked for, a towering fir, a patriarch among the trees that had been struck by lightning in years past. The bolt had split the crown of the fir down the middle and charred the wood. Nate remembered passing it shortly before he spotted the renegades.

With the golden crown of the sun creasing the eastern horizon, the wild creatures were stirring to life. Sparrows and finches chirped, chipmunks climbed onto logs and boulders to chatter and flick their tails, noisy squirrels were again abroad in the trees, and larger animals were coming out to forage.

To Nate, the many sounds were akin to listening to an orchestra tune its musical instruments before launching into a masterful composition. The creatures were likewise preparing for another active day of living out their lives in accordance with the melody of existence Nature had decreed for them. He breathed deep and smiled.

Nate's smile widened when he spied the split fir tree. "We're close," he announced, and made for a patch of underbrush 40 yards off. A low nicker sounded as he approached, and pushing past a bush he saw the black stallion and the other horses. "We did it," he told Clay Basket. "We're safe now."

"Is that a fact?" someone else responded, and from out of concealment stepped Roarke and two other renegades with their rifles cocked and leveled.

Chapter Twelve

Ira Galt put his hands on his hips and sneered at the defiant bound pair in front of him. "Did you really think you'd get away from us? Hell, we've been outfoxing fools like you for a couple of years now." So saying, he suddenly lashed out and slapped Nate King across the face.

The blow was so powerful that Nate staggered and would have fallen had he not bumped into Clay Basket, who stood firm. His cheek stung and he tasted blood on the tip of his tongue.

"That's for giving us such a hard time, you bastard," Galt said. Without warning, he swung again. "And that's for killing Johnny and stabbing poor George."

Nate's lower lip was split, the side of his head throbbing. Holding his head high, he refused to show any pain. Over by the bales of peltries he saw the renegade named George lying on blankets, glaring hatefully. There was no doubt what the killer would like to do to him.

Galt rested a hand on one of his pistols. "I should blow

your brains out, but that's too easy. You deserve to suffer for the aggravation you've caused us, to suffer like no one has ever suffered before."

"Cut off his oysters and cram them down his throat," suggested one of the men.

"There's a fine notion," Galt said, smirking.

"Stake him out and skin him alive," proposed another.

"Another good idea, Quince," Galt responded.

Roarke cleared his throat. "Give him to me. I know how to make him suffer." He chuckled. "I saw a prospector done in by the Comanches once. He'd had stakes driven into his arms and legs and slivers driven under his nails. Besides that, the red vermin gouged out his eyes and chopped off his ears and his nose. This polecat deserves the same treatment."

"Those Comanches can be so inventive," Galt said. Reaching out, he gripped Nate by the chin. "What do you think? Would you rather have us do it Quince's way or Roarke's?"

Nate remained silent.

"I asked you a question," Galt said, his grin transforming into a throaty growl as he brutally lashed out with his right fist.

Nate was helpless to dodge the blow. His stomach exploded in agony and he doubled over, wheezing noisily. Fingers twisted his hair and his head was yanked up.

"I want you to take days dying, Smith," Galt declared. "Days and days of torment, until you plead with me to end your rotten life. And when I'm done, maybe I'll make me a tobacco pouch from your hide and carry it with me wherever I go."

"Make me one too," Quince said.

"Say, ain't we forgettin' something?" said the last member of the gang, the one named Sterret. "What about those Blackfeet he mentioned? He claimed they were only a day or so behind him. They could show up at any time."

"I bet he was lying," Roarke said.

"Do we want to gamble all our pelts on whether he is or isn't?" Quince threw in.

All eyes were fixed on Nate. He had forgotten all about the yarn he had told, but now he saw a way of using it to delay his torture for a while, perhaps to even buy himself the whole day in which to devise a means of escaping. "I wasn't lying," he declared with fake conviction. "A war party will be here before you know it."

"Like hell!" Roarke snapped.

"Don't believe me. I don't care," Nate said. "I'd rather you stay here and get your hair lifted anyway. If I'm going to die, I want to take the whole bunch of you with me."

Bluff or fact? That was the crucial question Galt had to answer, and his puzzled expression showed he didn't know how he should take the assertion. "I'm inclined to go along with Roarke. You've already shown yourself to be a liar," he said. "You told us that you were afoot when you had horses hid nearby. You acted and talked like a damn greenhorn, but it's plain you're not. And you tried to take the Crow from us, which proves you know her."

"I never set eyes on her before I came into your camp," Nate stated.

"Then why'd you run off like you did?"

It was Clay Basket who answered. "That was my doing, Galt. I told him you were bad men out to hurt me, and I begged him to get me to safety."

"And he took your word just like that?" Galt said skeptically, snapping his fingers. "We hadn't done anything to him. Why should he believe you without proof?"

"What would you have done if you were in his place, alone among strangers?" Clay Basket shot back. "Walked up to them and demanded the truth?"

Galt's cloud of indecision darkened. He gazed westward, then at Nate, then at the peltries. "I still think you have a forked tongue, Smith, but I can't take the chance you're telling the truth. We've worked hard for our hides and we're not letting the Blackfeet or anyone else take them from us."

"We're pulling out?" Sterret asked.

"Yep. And we're taking these two with us."

"What about George? He's in no shape to ride."

The cutthroat in question overhead and called out, "You can't leave me here, Galt! It wouldn't be right. I'm entitled to my share and I aim to collect."

Roarke, Quince, and Galt walked over to their wounded companion and stood looking down at him. Nate glanced at Sterret, who was covering Clay Basket and him with a rifle, and decided not to try making a bid for freedom just yet.

"I mean it," George insisted. Coughing, he attempted to rise on an elbow but was too weak to do so. "We agreed we were all in this together, and we'd stick together through thick and thin."

Galt nodded. "That we did. But none of us counted on a situation like this cropping up. We can't let one man slow us down."

"I can keep up. Just get me on my horse."

"Who are you kidding? You couldn't sit a saddle in your condition."

"Damn it all, you can't up and desert me!" George said, a pitiable whine in his tone. "You owe it to me to take me along!"

"We owe you nothing," said Roarke.

"Not a thing," Quince added.

Sighing, Galt squatted and placed a hand on George's shoulder. "You can see the fix I'm in, can't you? If we stay to nursemaid you back to health, the Blackfeet might show up. We risk losing everything on account of you."

"But—" George began, and stopped when Galt raised a hand.

"I'm sorry, my friend. I truly am. If we could, I'd rig a travois and haul you to the Rendezvous. But doing so would delay us, let the Blackfeet overtake us. I owe it to the others not to let that happen."

"What are you saying?" George asked fearfully.

"We're going to have to leave you here with enough food and water to last you a while," Galt said. "If the Blackfeet don't show up in a day or two, we'll send someone back to stay with you."

"You lying scum!" George cried. "You will not! You'll leave me here to rot! And I'll be damned if I'll let you get away with it!" Infuriated, he tugged at a flintlock tucked under his belt, but in his feeble state he was unable to move very fast, and had yet to clear the barrel when there was a tremendous boom and his right temple burst outward in a spray of blood and flesh.

"You didn't give me any choice," Galt said, rising. He blew on the smoke curling from the end of his pistol, slid the flintlock under his belt, and grinned at his fellows. "I guess this means we divide up his share among us."

"More money for our pokes," Quince said.

Nate had seen too many men and women killed under much gorier circumstances to be very affected by the death of a murderous renegade trapper. He watched as George's companions stripped everything of value from the body and rolled it into high weeds. Then the cutthroats hastily loaded the stolen peltries onto the packhorses, threw their epishimores and saddles onto their mounts, and put out the fire. The preparations completed, the band gathered around the embers.

"I'm mighty surprised Belker ain't shown up yet," Sterret commented.

"What about it, Galt?" Roarke asked. "Are we going to wait for him or not?"

"You know how he is," Quince said before Galt could answer. "He told us he wasn't coming back until he tracked these two down, so he must still be out there beating the brush."

A suspicious glint lit Galt's gaze as he turned to Nate and the Crow woman. "The two of you wouldn't happen to have seen him, would you?"

"If I did, I'd have killed him," Nate said.

Several of the men laughed. "Kill Belker?" Sterret said. "Mister, the man ain't been born who can best him. He's tougher than a whole pack of Blackfeet and Bloods combined."

"He can take care of himself better than any man alive," Galt said. "So I say we ride on, but leave his horse here for him so he can catch up later."

"Yeah," Roarke said. "If he came back and didn't find his horse, he'd think we deserted him and likely hunt down each and every one of us, no matter how long it took." He paused. "I know that I sure as hell don't want him mad at me."

Even though there were now mounts to spare, Nate and Clay Basket had to ride double, Nate behind Quince, Clay Basket behind Galt. In single file the band moved out, each man leading pack animals. Quince was the last renegade in line, with three packhorses and the black stallion behind him.

Nate had to clamp his legs tight to keep from being thrown as the killers goaded their mounts into a trot and headed eastward through dense woodland. Immediately Nate began working his wrists back and forth, striving to loosen the rope binding them. His arms had been bent so sharply behind his back that his shoulders ached constantly, but he gritted his teeth against the discomfort and persevered.

The rope was terribly tight, chafing Nate's skin with every little movement. He hadn't been at it for five minutes when a trickle of blood ran down his wrist. Regardless, he continued straining and pulling and tugging. Whenever Quince glanced back, Nate froze. In this manner he went on for the better part of the morning, until his wrists and palms were slick with blood and the loops of rope had loosened a fraction.

Galt was canny about the route he took. Avoiding ridges and hills and high slopes, he stuck to the lowlands and the best cover. Plenty of practice had made him a master at avoiding detection, and he did all he could to throw the Blackfeet off the scent, including riding down the middle of a wide stream for over an hour.

Nate kept an eye on the sun. He expected the renegades to call a halt about midday to rest the horses, and he worried they would see the blood on his arms and realize what he had been up to. He had to free himself before they stopped.

In due course a spacious, verdant valley opened out before them. Buffalo grass waved in the wind, and at the far end of the valley was a small herd of mountain buffalo, shaggier counterparts of their brethren on the plains, grazing peacefully.

"Look yonder!" Sterret cried.

"Meat on the hoof," Roarke said. "What do you think, Galt? We haven't had fresh buffler meat in a coon's age. This child is plumb starved for some."

"Have you forgotten about the Blackfeet?" Galt responded.

"Blackfeet, hell," Roarke said. "We can camp over in the

trees and keep our fire low. If we keep our eyes peeled, they won't catch us napping."

Nate was secretly pleased when Galt agreed and the whole party rode to the right into the woods. A suitable clearing was soon found, and leaving Quince to serve as guard, the other three renegades galloped off after the buffalo. Nate contrived to always face the cutthroats so none got a look at his wrists, and as soon as the trio left, he set to work with a vengeance. He was on his knees, close to the pack animals. Beside him, on a stump, sat Clay Basket.

Quince paced back and forth a score of feet away. Now and then he would mutter to himself, often loud enough to be heard. "I don't like this, I don't like this one bit," he was saying. "Now isn't the time to be thinking of our stomachs, not with a war party in the area. No, we should be hightailing it for the Green River. To hell with a bunch of mangy buffalo!"

Nate saw the renegade shift to stare at him, and he stopped moving his arms. When Quince resumed pacing, he resumed the rubbing action that was steadily loosening the rope. By now he had almost a quarter of an inch leeway.

Clay Basket had noticed his efforts. She sat tense with anticipation, and when he looked at her, she smiled encouragement.

Suddenly Quince stopped pacing and came toward them.

Relaxing, Nate sank onto his buttocks and partially twisted his body so that he faced the grubby renegade. He feared Quince was going to check his wrists, but Quince walked on by. Nate twisted further, and almost laughed when the cutthroat rummaged in a parfleche on one of the pack animals and drew out a handful of jerked deer meat. "How about a bite for us?" Nate asked.

"Starve, bastard," Quince responded, taking a hearty bite

as he moved back across the clearing.

Rising on his knees once more, Nate worked harder than ever. He peered through the trees, but saw no sign of the rest of the renegades, who were probably circling around to get up close to the buffalo before firing. More blood dampened his wrists, making the ropes extremely slippery. He yanked hard, trying to wriggle a hand free.

Quince was standing still, staring off across the valley at the herd. "Hurry it up," he grumbled. "It doesn't take all damn day to drop a buffalo."

Inch by gradual inch Nate was freeing his right hand. The rope slowly slid down over the fleshy part hand above his thumb, gouging in deep as it did. Then it caught and wouldn't budge. His arms muscles became cords as he exerted all of his strength. There was excruciating pain and more blood flowed, but seconds later, his hand slipped completely out.

"Damn them," Quince still complained. "I have half a mind to ride off by myself and let them get themselves killed."

Freeing the left hand was easy. Nate flexed his fingers, restoring the circulation. Slowly, he rose into a crouch and padded forward, on the lookout for twigs and dry grass. He had to strike swiftly to prevent the renegade from giving a cry or getting off a shot that would bring the others back on the run.

"Galt is just too cocky," Quince groused. "That's always been his problem. He doesn't know when to stop pushing his luck."

Nate wiped his palms on his leggings as he closed the gap. His weapons had been divided up among the cut-throats, and if he remembered correctly Quince had one of his pistols. In addition, Quince had another pistol, a butcher knife, and a fine Kentucky rifle.

Only six feet separated Nate from the unsuspecting renegade when the unforeseen reared its unwanted head in the form of a chattering squirrel in the trees beyond the horses. One of the pack animals whinnied and shied, which caused Quince to glance over his shoulder. He saw Nate.

"What the hell!"

Nate King took a swift bound and leaped, his arms outstretched. He tackled Quince about the waist just as the cutthroat was bringing the Kentucky rifle to bear, and they both went down. Nate delivered a right to the jaw, or tried to, but his blow was deflected by the rifle barrel. He swung again, managed to connect with a glancing left, and then was rammed in the forehead by the Kentucky's stock. Pinwheels of light flickered before his eyes. Befuddled, he punched wildly. Something smashed him in the stomach, doubling him over, and the following instant he was bucked off and landed on his side.

"You're dead, you son of a bitch!" Quince rasped as he rose on one knee and began to take aim.

Since to lie there was to invite death, Nate did the only thing he could do; he went on the attack, surging up and springing even though he couldn't see the renegade clearly. His shoulder knocked the Kentucky to one side, and his fingers found purchase around Quince's skinny throat. Again they toppled. This time Nate was determined to finish his foe off.

Quince had other ideas. He pounded the Kentucky against Nate's chin, rocking Nate backward, but the fingers gouging into Quince's throat didn't let up. Frantic now, Quince released the rifle and groped at his waist for his knife. A single stroke was all it would take and the fight would be over.

Nate's vision was rapidly clearing. He felt rather than saw Quince's hand groping about under him, and he divined

Quince's intent. Letting go of the cutthroat's neck, he seized Quince's arm and rolled, pulling Quince's hand away from the knife hilt. Fiercely they struggled, Quince to get the knife, Nate to stop him, until changing tactics, Nate made a grab for the knife himself. His fingers closed on the smooth hilt and he began to draw the blade when Quince locked a hand on his wrist, pinning his arm in place.

For such a skinny man, Quince was endowed with exceptional strength. Or perhaps the excitement of the moment lent him more than his normal share. Whichever, he wrested Nate's hand from the knife and shoved, temporarily separating them and giving Quince time to reach for one of the pistols.

Nate lashed out with a knee, catching Quince in the groin. Gurgling, Quince scrambled backward, a hand over his privates. He pulled on the pistol, and almost had the flintlock out when Nate drove his knuckles into Quince's jaw, dazing him. Nate followed through with another fist, and saw the cutthroat go limp.

Thinking Quince was unconscious, Nate caught his breath while slowly rising. The Kentucky rifle lay a few feet away and he stepped over to it and bent down.

"Behind you!"

Clay Basket's yell brought Nate around barely in time. Quince had the knife out and was slashing the blade at his chest. Nate twisted sharply, feeling the keen edge slice into his shirt and nick his skin. His right hand closed on Quince's wrist and they grappled, dancing in a tight circle.

Nate saw his own flintlock on Quince's right hip. Breaking Quince's grasp on his arm, he snatched the pistol, cocking the piece as he did. Quince was elevating the knife for a death stroke.

"Die!"

The shriek ended in a gasp of surprise when Nate jammed

the pistol barrel into the renegade's stomach and squeezed the trigger. The muffled retort was no louder than a hand clap. Quince stiffened, whined, and clutched at himself.

Nate pushed to his feet and claimed the rifle. Another shot, however, wasn't in order as Quince was in the midst of his death throes, convulsing and blubbering as spittle frothed his lips. His wild gaze roved the clearing and settled on Nate.

"You . . . You . . ."

Whatever the cutthroat intended to say would remain a mystery. Exhaling all the air in his lungs, Quince wordlessly moved his lips, his fingers formed into claws, and he died.

Nate checked for a pulse to be certain. Once he was, he scooped up the knife, hurried to Clay Basket, and cut her loose. "Thanks for the warning."

"Did the others hear the shot?"

If they had, Nate had no way of knowing, for a survey of the lower end of the valley revealed only the buffalo. The renegades were still hidden in the trees. "You have to leave now," he advised. "Take Quince's horse and head west."

"What about you?"

"I have a score to settle."

"Not alone."

"There's a time and a place for being stubborn and this isn't it," Nate said, taking her elbow and propelling her toward the mounts. "I can't fight them and worry about you at the same time."

"You have done much for me, Grizzly Killer. I will not leave you when you need my help."

"What about Nelson?" Nate tried a new tack. "He needs you too, more than I do. He needs doctoring real bad. Head on back to where you saw him last and lend my friends a hand."

"No," Clay Basket said, digging in her heels.

"Damn it all," Nate huffed. "I don't want you hurt."

"I am staying."

Arguing was a luxury Nate could ill afford since he had no idea of how soon the other renegades would show up. "All right," he said in compromise, "you can stay provided you keep low while I do what needs doing."

"Give me a gun and I will fight alongside you."

"You'll do no such thing." Nate walked to Quince and retrieved the butcher knife and Quince's powder horn and ammo pouch. He reloaded the spent pistol, then verified the second flintlock and the Kentucky were loaded. Armed to the teeth, he stepped to the horses and cut the black stallion loose. The whole time Clay Basket anxiously watched him.

"I am Crow, not Osage," she mentioned, referring to a tribe whose members were notoriously inept at fighting. "I have fought the Blackfeet and the Sioux when they raided our village. I am no coward."

"Never claimed you were," Nate responded. "But these are whites. I'm white. We'll let it go at that." He swung up and wheeled the stallion, but could go no further because she blocked his path.

"For the last time," Clay Basket pleaded.

A jab of Nate's heels, a flick of the reins, and he was past her and crossing the clearing. He drew up halfway across to look around. She hadn't moved. "Get on Quince's horse and go off into the brush. If I go down, you know what to do."

"You lied, Grizzly Killer."

"What?"

"Your skin is white but inside you are one of us."

Those words rang in Nate's ears as he rode to the edge of the trees. At last he spied one of the renegades, the man

named Sterret, creeping through the grass at the far end of
the valley toward the two dozen or so buffalo. Evidently
the cutthroats had circled completely around the herd to
get between the hulking brutes and the nearest forest. That
way, if the buffalo spooked, they'd be able to drop one or
two before the herd reached cover.

Nate brought the stallion to a gallop, hugging the tree
line. He hoped Galt and Roarke were also in the high grass.
In one fell swoop he could wipe out all three if they didn't
spot him first.

A tall bull on the west flank of the herd lifted its huge
head to stare at the still-distant stallion. The bull showed
no alarm and stood munching on the sweet grass.

Bending low so his outline would blend into that of
the horse, Nate whipped the stallion to go faster. Buffalo were unpredictable creatures, like grizzlies. Sometimes
they'd flee at the drop of a feather, while at other times
they'd belligerently stand their ground against all comers.
They were less likely to flee from men on horseback if
they couldn't see the men, no doubt because they had no
ingrained fear of horses. This was why many Indians had
learned to swing onto the sides of their mounts as they
approached herds and then rear up at the last instant to
loose their arrows, thus taking their quarry unawares.

Nate intended to do the same. He rode another hundred
yards along the edge of the trees, shifted onto the off-side
of the stallion, and broke into the open, making straight for
the herd. Peeking past the animal's neck, he could see more
and more of the buffalo staring at the onrushing horse. None
displayed any alarm, yet.

A buffalo was a massive engine of destruction. Standing six feet high at the shoulders, weighing well over a
thousand pounds in many instances, and endowed with
wicked, curved horns boasting a spread of three feet, it

was capable of bowling over and goring a horse or a man with equal ease. Multiply that by dozens, or hundreds, or many thousands, and it was understandable why anything or anyone that got in the path of a fleeing herd was reduced to so much pulp and broken bone.

Nate was counting on this particular herd to do the job he had to do for him. He galloped ever nearer, until he was within 30 yards of the foremost bull. Then, straightening, he vented a series of piercing war whoops that would have done justice to a full-blooded Shoshone. Simultaneously he waved his rifle and flapped his arms.

The effect on the herd was instantaneous. As one the mighty beasts spun and fled, their heavy hoofs pounding the ground in a thunderous staccato beat. Bulls, cows, and calves alike sped eastward as if the valley was on fire and flames nipped at their tails.

Beyond the herd, Sterret leaped erect. Panic lined his features as he whirled and raced toward the sanctuary of the forest, but he was closer to the buffalo than the trees and the buffalo were much faster than he was. He glanced back repeatedly, his eyes wide, his mouth agape, and when it became apparent the herd would be upon him in the next few seconds, he turned and fired at the nearest animal, a large bull. The single shot had no effect.

Nate saw Sterret throw up his arms, heard the man's wavering scream. The renegade tried to dodge the bull but failed, and he screamed louder as a slashing horn ripped into his stomach and he was hurled high into the air. Sterret came down on his back directly in front of a compact mass of buffalo. A final scream was torn from his throat just as he disappeared under their flailing hooves.

Eagerly Nate scanned the grass, hoping both Galt and Roarke would be caught in the stampede. He spotted a figure in the trees, fleeing toward a waiting horse, but couldn't tell which one of them it was. The horse panicked and ran, stranding the figure, who quickly darted to a nearby tree and began climbing with the alacrity of a squirrel. Moments later the herd swept by, snapping saplings and flattening brush. The thin tree swayed as the man clung for dear life.

Nate was 50 yards out when the tree broke and went down. There was no sound from the man as he fell. The clouds of dust being raised by the buffalo prevented Nate from seeing whether the renegade had been trampled. He rode to the tree line and leaped off while the stallion was still in motion, diving behind the trunk of a pine.

By now the herd was lost in the maze of trees, but the diminishing din of their passage told of their continued flight. Nate covered his mouth to keep from coughing as the dust settled around him. He focused on the spot where the renegade had gone down, but could see no body.

Cautiously, Nate worked his way forward, going from trunk to trunk. The odds were still against him and he had to have eyes in the back of his head if he wanted to stay alive. Galt and Roarke would slay him on sight.

Suddenly a rifle cracked, the lead ball smacking into the trunk inches from Nate's head. He went prone, saw puffs of gunsmoke off to the right, and twisted to aim. A buckskin-clad figure appeared for just a heartbeat, then was gone.

Nate changed position too, dashing to another tree, one with a wider trunk. His eyes raked the undergrowth to no avail. A glance back confirmed he was safe from that direction, for the moment at least.

A hint of motion near a boulder heralded another sharp retort. This time slivers stung Nate's cheek and he ducked down, the Kentucky pressed to his shoulder. But whoever had fired had vanished.

Easing onto his stomach, Nate crawled to his right, closer
to the boulder rather than away from it. He slanted behind
a waist-high bush and paused to scour the general vicinity.
About 25 yards off a man materialized next to a tree. It
was Roarke, and he was staring at the spot Nate had just
vacated. Nate slowly brought the Kentucky rifle up. The
.40-caliber rifle was less powerful than his Hawken, but
a bit more accurate at longer ranges thanks to its longer
barrel. At this close distance, aligning the front and rear
sights was child's play. Nate took a bead on the center of
Roarke's chest, and when the cutthroat leaned a bit further
out to look for him, he gently stroked the trigger.

Roarke toppled backward, the rifle he held flying. He
crashed onto his back, tried to stand, and collapsed.

Drawing his pistol, Nate sprinted across the intervening
space, then halted as Roarke attempted again to rise. Roarke
spotted him and made as if to draw a flintlock. "Don't!"
Nate warned.

But Roarke paid no heed. His hand was closing on his
pistol when Nate's pistol blasted and a second ball cored
his chest, knocking him flat. Coughing uncontrollably, he
spat blood and feebly tried to sit up.

Several rapid strides brought Nate to the cutthroat. He
slammed down a foot on Roarke's pistol, pinning the gun
to the ground. There were two holes in the renegade's
chest, side by side, from which crimson stream poured.
Roarke tried to speak but produced only a strangled whis-
per. "Where's Galt?" Nate demanded.

"Go . . . to . . . hell," Roarke croaked, and died, vindic-
tive to the last.

Nate lowered into a crouch and picked up the rifle Roarke
had dropped, which was his own Hawken. He checked
it, set down the Kentucky, and commenced reloading his
pistol, all the while gazing around about him. There was

still Galt to deal with, and he had to be ready.

Total silence shrouded the forest. The buffalo were long gone, and the birds and lesser creatures had either fled or sought shelter in their burrows or elsewhere.

For the time being Nate left the Kentucky and Roarke's other weapons where they were and moved into the brush. Taking a seat on a log, he waited and listened, confident that if Galt was sneaking up on him, he would detect the renegade first. But there were no sounds to be heard; there was no movement anywhere. Close to ten minutes went by, and the only thing Nate saw was a solitary butterfly fluttering among some flowers.

Standing, Nate warily advanced to the edge of the high grass. He entertained the notion that Galt must have been trampled along with Sterret, and with that in mind he moved into the open seeking Galt's body. Hoofprints and droppings were everywhere. Wide tracts of grass had been crushed flat by the stampede, making his search a bit easier.

Presently Nate came on Sterret, or what was left of the renegade. As he stood staring down at an eyeball that was being swarmed over by ants, he caught a faint glint of sunlight on metal out of his right eye. Nate spun, bending at the knees as he did. There was the bang of a rifle and a hornet buzzed his ear. He promptly replied in kind.

To the south, 60 yards away, Ira Galt was perched in the low fork of a mountain alder. At the crack of the Hawken a scarlet spray gushed from the back of his skull and he threw out his arms in involuntary reflex. Slowly he did an ungainly pirouette. Then his foot slipped and he plummeted to the earth. He made no effort to rise, not even when a small leaf, dislodged by his fall, fluttered from above and landed in his open mouth.

Nate King saw the leaf when he reached the body. "You're

the one who got off too easy," he said gruffly as he took Galt's weapons and turned to go. Then he paused. "This is for all those you butchered." Drawing back his right leg, he kicked Galt full in the face. "May you rot in hell."

Epilogue

Nate King and Clay Basket spent the rest of the day riding westward. They were only a few miles past the basin when they met Pepin, sent ahead by a very worried Shakespeare McNair to see how Nate was faring. Nate asked Pepin to bring the pack animals and pushed on, relying once again on the Comanche trick of often changing horses to cover the miles swiftly. It was well after midnight when a small fire in the narrow valley came into view.

Clay Basket was first on the ground. Her face aglow, she ran to the man lying by the fire and threw her arms around him, tears flowing down her smooth cheeks as she smothered him with kisses.

Tim Nelson had been sleeping. He awoke with a start, saw who was holding him, and added his tears of joy to hers.

"You're alive, my love!" Clay Basket declared.

"And he'll stay that way, if you don't squeeze him to death," Shakespeare McNair said, grinning. "That man of yours has an iron constitution. That and the herbs I've given him have pulled him through. He'll be laid up for quite a spell, but he'll be good as new in time."

"Thank you," Clay Basket said, gazing warmly at the grizzled mountain man, then at Nate, on whom her eyes lingered. "For everything."

WILDERNESS

Fang & Claw
David Thompson

To survive in the untamed wilderness a man needs all the friends he can get. No one can battle the continual dangers on his own. Even a fearless frontiersman like Nate King needs help now and then and he's always ready to give it when it's needed. So when an elderly Shoshone warrior comes to Nate asking for help, Nate agrees to lend a hand. The old warrior knows he doesn't have long to live and he wants to die in the remote canyon where his true love was killed many years before, slain by a giant bear straight out of Shoshone myth. No Shoshone will dare accompany the old warrior, so he and Nate will brave the dreaded canyon alone. And as Nate soon learns the hard way, some legends are far better left undisturbed.

___4862-0 $3.99 US/$4.99 CAN

LANCASTER'S ORPHANS
Robert J. Randisi

It certainly isn't what Lancaster had expected. When he rode into Council Bluffs, he thought he would just stop at the bar for a beer. How could he know he'd ride right into the middle of a lynching? Lancaster can't let an innocent man be hanged, but when the smoke clears and the lynching stops, a bystander lies dying on the ground, caught in the crossfire. With his last breath he asks Lancaster to take care of the people who had been depending on him—a wagon train filled with women and children on their way to California!

MIRACLE
OF THE
JACAL
ROBERT J. RANDISI

Elfego Baca is a young lawman—but he already has a reputation. He is known to be good with a gun. Very good. And he is known to never back down, especially if he is fighting for something he believes in. This reputation has spread far and wide throughout his home territory of New Mexico. Sometimes it works in his favor, sometimes it works against him. But there will come a day when his reputation will not only be tested, but expanded—a day when young Elfego will have to prove just how good with a gun he really is . . . and how brave. It will be a day when he will have to do the impossible and live through it. For a long time afterward, people will still be talking about the miracle of the *jacal*.

___4923-6 $4.99 US/$5.99 CAN

RAIDERS OF THE WESTERN & ATLANTIC
TIM CHAMPLIN

Young Josiah Waymeier, a private in the 2nd Ohio Volunteer Infantry, has been chosen to be part of a daring and dangerous plan. A select group of Union soldiers attempts to steal the *General* behind enemy lines and drive the engine straight to safety in Union territory, burning Confederate bridges as they go. Meanwhile, Josiah's mother intends to steal a shipment of gold bullion from the Confederacy and take it to a rendezvous with the *General,* to contribute the money to the Union cause. When the theft of the engine unleashes a desperate pursuit through Confederate territory, both mother and son find themselves racing not only to perform their missions, but for their very lives!

THE DEVIL'S
CORRAL
LES SAVAGE, JR.

The three short novels in this thrilling collection are among the finest written by Les Savage, Jr., one of the true masters of Western fiction. The Devil in *The Devil's Corral* is a stubborn horse that has never allowed anyone to ride him. Even worse, Devil puts Ed Ketland in the hospital and gives him a fear of horses, a fear he has to overcome one way or another. *Satan Sits a Big Bronc* is set in Texas shortly before the War Between the States, where a carpetbag governor organizes a group of hardcases to enforce his new laws. And in *Senorita Scorpion*, Chisos Owens is offered one thousand dollars to find the mysterious Scorpion, but his reasons have nothing to do with the reward.